Gwen Molnar

HATE CELL

A CASEY TEMPLETON MYSTERY

DUNDURN PRESS
TORONTO

Copyright: Gwen Molnar, 2009

Editor: Michael Carroll
Design: Jennifer Scott
Printer: Webcom

Library and Archives Canada Cataloguing in Publication

Molnar, Gwen
    Hate cell / by Gwen Molnar.

(A Casey Templeton mystery)
ISBN 978-1-55002-850-8

    I. Title. II. Series: Molnar, Gwen. Casey Templeton mystery.

PS8576.O4515H38 2008   jC813'.54   C2008-906213-2

1 2 3 4 5   13 12 11 10 09

   ONTARIO ARTS COUNCIL
CONSEIL DES ARTS DE L'ONTARIO

We acknowledge the support of **The Canada Council for the Arts** and the **Ontario Arts Council** for our publishing program. We also acknowledge the financial support of the **Government of Canada** through the **Book Publishing Industry Development Program** and **The Association for the Export of Canadian Books**, and the **Government of Ontario** through the **Ontario Book Publishers Tax Credit** program, and the **Ontario Media Development Corporation**.

Care has been taken to trace the ownership of copyright material used in this book. The author and the publisher welcome any information enabling them to rectify any references or credits in subsequent editions.

J. Kirk Howard, President

Printed and bound in Canada.
Printed on recycled paper.
www.dundurn.com

Dundurn Press
3 Church Street, Suite 500
Toronto, Ontario, Canada
M5E 1M2

Gazelle Book Services Limited
White Cross Mills
High Town, Lancaster, England
LA1 4XS

Dundurn Press
2250 Military Road
Tonawanda, NY
U.S.A. 14150

To my beloved family —
husband, George;
daughter, Jane; son, Charles;
and granddaughter, Hazel.

ACKNOWLEDGEMENTS

Grateful thanks for the insights and editorial assistance of Dale Anderson, Brenda Bellingham, Barbara Cram, Joy Gugeler, John McGregor, and Connie Shupe. And I would like to especially recognize the help and support of Daniel Kline and Alberta Searle.

CHAPTER ONE

"I should go back," Casey Templeton muttered to himself. "I could do it tomorrow." But he kept walking through the dark, empty streets as a cool fall breeze changed rapidly to a cold winter wind. Then he stopped and put down his flashlight. "Oh, what the heck!"

Casey zipped his coat, pulling up the collar so snow wouldn't get down his neck, then tugged his knitted hat over his forehead. He patted his pockets for gloves. No gloves. It wouldn't take that long, he reassured himself, and then he would be done with this necessary chore.

It wasn't the bitter wind that made Casey hesitate, or even that he was scared ... exactly. There

were things going on lately that made almost everyone uncomfortable, things people couldn't understand. Things that had turned the safe, comfortable town of Richford, Alberta, into a place
where fear reigned.

Why pick on Mr. Finegood and his family? Casey
thought as he trudged into the gloom. *And why do
such ugly things to the Olbergs? I just don't get it.*

He crossed the silent railway tracks. The tow-
ering grain elevator beside the tracks loomed dark
and unfriendly. He hurried past it and almost ran
until he reached the last street on the north edge of
town, a street where the new houses were less and
less complete as he got nearer the final streetlamp.
A heavier snow had begun to fall. He wished now
he had told his brother, Hank, where he was going,
or had left a note or something. As it was, nobody
knew, and the farther he got from home the more
uneasy he felt.

At the last streetlight he turned and glanced back.
All was still. His footprints in the snow disappeared in
shadowy retreat beyond the golden glow of the light.
If the snow kept up, his footsteps would completely
disappear and there would be no trace he had walked
this way. Never mind. Once he had realized where
he had lost his dad's antique pipe, he had promised
himself he would go back to the Old Willson with Two
Ls Place and get it. Casey always tried to keep vows,
even to himself, especially to himself, like now. He
would rather get the pipe no matter what happened
than face the music if his dad noticed it wasn't in its

glass case. Now, as he trudged through the swirling snow, he cast his mind back to the sequence of events that had brought him here.

Once again, here in Richford, Casey was the new kid and on the outside. It never really bothered him anymore not being accepted right away. It was a lot better than, say, a kid like Bryan Ogilvy, who had lived his whole life in Richford and was such an outsider that the other kids totally ignored him. Bryan was just there. Even most of the teachers hardly ever talked to him. Casey couldn't understand why everyone was so mean to Bryan, so he went out of his way to say hello to Bryan whenever their paths crossed, which wasn't often because Bryan didn't play any sports or belong to any clubs and faded away after school. But Bryan and Casey both liked science, and they had teamed up on a science project.

Casey had learned a lot about the new kid role, knew you never let them know you were lonely. You just did your own thing and played it very, very cool. A way to become an insider would always come up if you didn't push, if you stood back, listened, and bided your time. Take today for instance. He had heard Kevin Schreiver and Terry Bracco talking when he was in the little storage closet putting away the basketballs after gym. Casey had been at the school long enough to know that Kevin and Terry were the kind of guys he would like for friends.

"I got six cigarettes now," Kevin said. "How about we go to the Old Willson Place right after school?"

"Sure, we gotta try smoking sometime, but I have to walk Butch first," Terry said.

"Bring Butch along," Kevin suggested. "Tie him up while we smoke."

Casey kept quiet until they were gone. While he waited he planned. He would dash home after school, get his dad's fancy old pipe, fill it with tobacco from some of Hank's cigarettes, and be out at the Old Willson Place sitting on the porch, smoking the pipe by the time Kevin and Terry got there with Butch. It worked perfectly. He could tell they were impressed with him sitting there gazing off into the woods, pipe in hand. They didn't need to know what a terrible time he'd had lighting it and that he'd really taken only one puff. They didn't even take out their cigarettes, just said they had come out to the old place to look around.

Inside the Old Willson Place, Casey pulled a big bottle of Sprite and a package of chocolate chip cookies from his backpack. The three sat on piles of grubby pillows in the living room and started in with the stories about Mr. Clarence Wilberforce Willson with Two Ls, as he *always* pointed out to *everyone*. Lucky there were no Willsons with only one *l* in town, thought Casey. They would have suffered a terrible inferiority complex. Clarence Willson was still Richford's most famous citizen, though he had been dead for more than eighty years. Both the local library and the high school had been named after him.

Kevin and Terry had a lot of stories about the Willsons, but Casey had some they had never heard because Casey's great-grandfather had been a type-setter for Mr. Willson's *Richford Weekly Mirror* way back in 1900 or something. The stories from those days had been passed down to the newest generation of Templetons. Sure, Kevin and Terry knew about the body that had been found in the attic whose door had two heavy pieces of wood crossed over it and nailed down to keep people out, but they had never heard that three of Old Willson's babies had died of scarlet fever on three mid-April days in 1906. The terrible loss had driven Mrs. Willson into a deep depression from which she never recovered. Casey said it was her ghost that walked the grounds on those three mid-April days each year.

As he pulled open the drapes covering the living-room windows to get more light, it crossed Casey's mind that they seemed new compared with the stained and faded pillows they were sitting on.

"Time to get back." Terry stood and brushed dust from his pants. "You want to come over to the Rec Hall later, Casey? Kevin and I go there Friday nights."

"Thanks a lot," Casey said. "Can't tonight, but maybe another Friday, okay?" Never seem too eager. That was the secret. Let them get the idea you were worth waiting for.

"Sure," Kevin said. "Let's go."

It must have been when they were standing up that the pipe he had put in his coat pocket had fallen among the pillows.

It was just plain luck that his parents had gone out to Jim Bailey's house to play bridge right after supper. Hank and Casey had cleaned up the kitchen — a job you did if there were four boys in the family and your dad was in the Royal Canadian Mounted Police. "Might as well get used to a little KP, boys," his father always said. "Your mother works hard enough making the meals." KP? Nobody in Richford except some old war veterans probably knew that it stood for "kitchen police," that it meant you got to do everything in the kitchen and leave it "like nobody lived there," as his father was fond of saying.

Hank was at his computer. He was always at his computer. He had won the whole setup — computer, printer, scanner, and about a dozen games — at the draw at the new grocery store in the "big" new mall. Big? Well, it was for Richford. But, hey, Casey had seen malls almost as big as the whole town of Richford — like West Edmonton Mall. Now *that* was a mall — biggest in the world, they said. But nobody in the family had ever won anything there, and here was Hank, not two months in Richford, and he had won first prize in the draw. A person had to be sixteen to enter. That left Casey out by two years.

Casey had been born long after Hank when nobody in the family had expected there would be another baby. After three sons, Jake now twenty-four, Billy twenty-one, both at university, and Hank eighteen and a half, his parents likely wished, when they knew there was going to be another child, that it would be a girl. But instead along came Knightly Charles (after his two grandfathers' middle names),

14

always and forever after to be called KC, then Casey, white-blond and blue-eyed from day one. For about a week at each new school, people called him Knightly, and for some strange reason that suited Casey just fine. But once they got wind of his nickname, he was Casey to everyone.

Since the death of Hank's girlfriend, Cindy, two years earlier — she had been sick only two days when she died of meningitis — Hank had only two things he cared about: his twenty-year-old Harley-Davidson motorcycle and his computer. Casey heard his parents arguing over it all the time. His mom usually said something like, "Colin, nagging isn't going to help. Hank's still hurting. One day he'll re-member that there's more in life than the Internet and the Harley. Trust me."

They had all liked Cindy a lot. She was tall, with masses of honey-coloured hair, sparkly dark brown eyes, and a great smile. She was smart and fun and so easy to be with. They didn't talk about it much, but they missed her.

Casey knew if he said good-night and went up to his room, Hank would hardly take any notice. So he did just that. Hank muttered something but didn't even turn around. As Casey tucked his pillow un-der the duvet in case Hank did check on him in bed, he wondered how much time he would need to find his dad's pipe and get back. An hour and a half, two hours max should do it. He went quietly downstairs, picked his coat and hat off the hook, put on his boots, took his dad's flashlight, and silently opened and closed the back door. Standing on the porch for a minute, he waited to see if Hank had heard anything. Then he headed off. It was starting to snow a bit, and the sky had the reddish cloudy cast it had when a heavy snowstorm was brewing.

He had heard all about the red snow sky on the Prairies, and how some years, heavy snow began falling as early as the first week of October. It seemed as if this would be one of those years.

There wasn't much about the Prairies winter, summer, spring, or fall that he hadn't heard before from his parents. And they had finally gotten their wish to come back to Richford, "Paradise on the Prairies," their hometown.

"Don't know where I'd call my hometown," Casey muttered now as he continued to trudge through the snow to the Willson Place. He went over in his mind the six or so places he had lived so far. He was sure of one thing. He didn't want to go back to the last one — Edmonton. There were too many bad family memories back there. He recalled the day his dad had gone off to Afghanistan in the first rotation of a Canadian commitment under the North Atlantic Treaty Organization. The Mounties' role was to help train new recruits for the Afghan national police. Casey's father had done a similar tour of duty in Bosnia in the 1990s. In Afghanistan, though, his dad had been seriously injured by an improvised explosive device embedded in a country road. Although he had fully recovered, the incident had played a part in his early retirement.

And now Richford, the paradise his parents had remembered so fondly, wasn't so great anymore. Now the Finegoods, the only Jewish family in town, had had a pipe bomb thrown at their store window, and Mrs. Olberg's sister-in-law, Maria McKay, a Gypsy from Romania, had been knocked down and almost run over when she was crossing the street near where she lived. A van with smoked windows, which witnesses said had its licence plate taped over, left her on the road and roared away as a bunch of leaflets were tossed out its window. Casey's mom had picked up one. It listed reasons why Gypsies shouldn't be allowed to exist, never mind live, in Richford.

Casey couldn't explain why he felt compelled to get his dad's pipe back tonight. It wasn't as if his father was overly strict with Hank or Casey. It was more a feeling that Casey had of not wanting to let his dad down, especially since his father was such an upright kind of guy who never seemed to make a false move or do anything just for the fun of it.

Actually, Casey now thought, he didn't really know his father all that well. His dad had been gone for so much of his life. Walking on, he considered that fact and wondered if he was a stranger to his father, too. Casey would have bet that his dad didn't know what he liked to read or listen to. Correction. His dad had to know what Casey listened to because he was always telling him to turn his music down. And Casey figured his father must have guessed by now that he loved to read fantasy. Likewise, Casey knew his dad liked biographies since he dragged them home from the library by the armful. And both of his parents liked jazz and classical music.

Hank was always telling Casey he should relax around their father the way Hank did, but somehow he couldn't. He was always doing something his father didn't approve of, or if his dad did approve, he was doing it the wrong way. Maybe, he thought now, one day he would do *something* right.

Casey had tried last week. He had thought he would surprise his dad by reorganizing his tool bench, but the favour hadn't been appreciated. Oh, well ...

He remembered only vaguely when the Templetons had lived for four years in Regina. All the boys were at home and their dad worked downtown. They saw him every night at supper, and though Casey had been just a little kid, he could still picture his dad hitting fly balls to his older brothers and shooting baskets with them. Not with Casey, though. Never. He couldn't think of a time when they had even gone for a walk together.

Casey thought how different his relationship with his mother was. She was always there for him and drove him all over the place so he wouldn't miss a single swim meet. His mother went to all the PTA meetings at every school he had ever attended, and what was more, she loved and understood him and gave him a little slack. Casey wished his dad were a little more lovable and a little less perfect.

When he got to the edge of the field near the Old Willson Place, he looked across it and stopped cold. A faint light shone from the old house's window, the window whose new drapes he had opened after school. As he watched, the light moved and went out.

It took all his courage to start across the field, but he soon halted again to shine the flashlight on his watch. He had already used up twenty-five minutes. Hurrying didn't help. He couldn't go any faster because of the deep furrows. Up, down, up, down — the field seemed endless. Walking sideways didn't help, either. His legs weren't long enough to step up and over the furrows, and twice he sat down heavily astride humps of frozen earth.

Then walking suddenly became easier. He had made it to the tree-lined road leading to the house. Not far to go now. Casey switched the flashlight to his right hand and pushed his left hand deep into his coat pocket to warm it. He had done quite a few dumb things in his life, but nothing as dumb as this. Hoping to glimpse the Willson gate, Casey held the flashlight as far as he could to his right. At the very moment he caught sight of the gate, his foot hit something unyielding on the path and he fell heavily into the snow, his flashlight cartwheeling away.

Casey lay stunned for a moment, then sat up and slid over to a dim halo of light under the snow a metre or so ahead. He turned the flashlight back to see what had tripped him. Casey could make out a lump in the snow but couldn't see what it was. He shone the light up higher. Above the snow were the tops of a pair of hiking boots, jean-clad legs, a heavy dark jacket with a high collar, and ... nothing. *Nothing?* Casey leaped up. Now he could see a man's head tilting so far back over the hinge edge of a wide chain-link gate that the face was thick with snow.

Pulling at the man's sleeve, Casey said, "Hey? Sir?"

The man's head swung slowly forward onto his chest. Before Casey could move away, the body fell against him, taking him down with it.

CHAPTER TWO

Casey could breathe, but could he free himself? By digging the heel of his right boot into the gravel under the snow, he was able to push up and slide a little. It took ages, but he finally made it, picked up his flashlight, and shone it on the man's face.

"Mr. Deverell!" What the heck was his science teacher doing out here?

Remembering that he should press his fingers on the thumb side of the wrist, Casey felt for Mr. Deverell's pulse. There was one, but it was faint and irregular. He took off his coat and folded it for a pillow. His hand slipped as he lifted his teacher's head, and his fingers came away sticky. He shone the light on his hand — blood!

Casey covered the distance between the gate and the front door in seconds. He beamed his light around the big front room, knowing he needed something to pull Mr. Deverell back to the house so the man could defrost. A big piece of cardboard would do, but there was nothing like that. And there was nothing in the kitchen or in the unfinished lean-to behind the kitchen.

Back in the living room, Casey swung the light around again, more slowly this time. The drapes! He yanked them down, sending their hooks flying, gathered them in a ball, and rushed out. Casey put his coat back on, spread one of the drapes beside the unconscious man, and rolled him onto it. Tucking the other drape around Mr. Deverell, Casey grabbed the two corners under his teacher's head, lifted them off the ground, and pulled. There was enough snow so that the improvised "sleigh" glided easily up to the steps. But now what? The pillows! He could shove one under Mr. Deverell's head, one under his middle, and one under his legs, then build them up until he got the man high enough to pull into the room. As he lifted two pillows, his dad's pipe rolled onto the floor. With relief Casey pocketed it and hurried out.

With his bloodstained coat back on, sweat poured down inside his shirt and cooled as Casey strained to lift the heavy man higher and higher on the pillows. Every time he got the feet up one pillow height a leg fell or, at the head end, an arm. When he finally had Mr. Deverell elevated enough, he spread a drape on the porch, rolled him onto it, and dragged the man into the house.

It wasn't all that much warmer inside than out, but Casey knew that was good, not bad. He had read somewhere that heating someone with hypothermia too fast was dangerous. Still, he had to heat Mr. Deverell somewhat, and the only way to do it was to get a blaze going in the fireplace. Since there was no cardboard around to start a fire, he had to use the chocolate-chip cookie bag he had left on the kitchen counter earlier in the day, as well as other scraps of paper on the floor. Casey had noticed that the unfinished lean-to had rough wooden slats tacked over tarpaper. He pried off six or seven and broke them in two across his knee.

Casey fumbled for the matches he had used to light his dad's pipe. Had it only been a few hours ago? It seemed like a month. There were only three left in the Ducks and Drakes matchbook he had scooped up from Hank's desk. Ducks and Drakes was Richford's premier café and Hank's favourite hangout.

One precious match went out as he tried to light the cookie package he had put under the broken slats in the fireplace. The red corrugated plastic cookie divider flared briefly, then went out. Casey crunched up all the bits of paper he had found into a loose ball and lit an edge of paper with his last match. It smouldered, seemed to die, then flared again. The ragged break of a slat caught fire, and in seconds all the wood started burning as smoke and ash billowed back into the room. Coughing, sputtering, and calling himself an idiot for not thinking of the flue, Casey pushed through the smoke and pressed it open. The smoke swept back and roared up the chimney as the fire burned even more quickly.

The smell would probably be awful, but all Casey could think to put on the flames were the drapes. He eased one from under Mr. Deverell, bunched it loosely, and held a corner to the fire until it ignited. It gave off a lot of heat.

If he packed pillows around Mr. Deverell, he could use the other drape, too. Casey looked around. "Yikes!" he shouted. The pillows outside were getting wet. Back out on the porch, he whacked pillows together, getting off all the snow he could, then returned to the fire and packed them close to and on top of his teacher.

It was time to concentrate on the still-unconscious Mr. Deverell. Was his pulse a little stronger? Casey hoped so, but he couldn't be certain. His teacher needed medical help, and soon. Casey didn't figure he should leave him alone for as long as it would take to get back to town, and for the ambulance to get from town to the Old Willson Place by the back road it would have to take.

He had read that sometimes there were boxes on top of remote telephone poles that linemen used to call for supplies. Taking the flashlight, Casey went out to the gate and craned his neck. He could barely make out the top of the pole and couldn't see if a box was there. And, anyway, how would he be able to climb up to get at it? There might not be a box, but there was a heavy, snow-crested wire sagging from the top of the pole to the house. Casey walked back under it. It looked as if the wire entered the house above a boarded-up attic window. But there was no electricity in the house — never had been since C. Wilberforce Willson had ripped it out when his grieving wife had finally taken her own life by electrocuting herself.

Back in the house, Casey put the second drape on the fire, then shone his light on the door to the attic. The heavy oak boards crossing over the door were too solid for him to remove, but as he slid a hand along one of the boards, something struck him as odd. Where there used to be nails holding the oak board, there were now screws. And the place where one of the screw heads showed was exactly over a gap between the door and the wall. The shaft of a long brass screw, the kind of screw Casey and Bryan had had a hard time finding for their science project last month, went straight into the gap, not into anything solid. He bent down and scrutinized the screw directly below it. Same thing. He reached through the crosspiece for the partly covered doorknob and yanked. The door, crosspieces and all, swung open, and Casey shone the light up as he negotiated the steep and narrow attic steps.

He saw a light switch on a pillar at the top of the steps and turned it on. The switch was connected to a four-way plug attached to one of two heavy black cables that came through the outer wall of the house above the boarded-up window. A small electric baseboard heater that radiated a bit of warmth was plugged into the same outlet as were a computer, printer, and scanner sitting on a square double desk in the centre of the room. Also on the double desk were a fax machine, DVD player, and videotape machine. Casey had heard Hank talking about "phone phreaks" who could tap into telephone company test lines. He figured they were at work here.

The room was like the RCMP strategy room his dad had once taken the Templeton family through. Like that room, this one was painted pale yellow green. The walls were lined with wide shelves on which leaflets, posters, catalogues, newspapers, videotapes, audiotapes, CDs, DVDs, and books were stacked, with bulging cardboard cartons pushed under the lower shelves.

One of the pamphlets was identical to those everyone in town had found about a month ago either stuck behind their car windshield wipers or in their mailboxes. They were full of biblical quotes and said bad things about gays and lesbians.

Casey picked up a poster. It read HONK IF YOU HATE GYPSIES. Another declared THE HOLOCAUST IS A HOAX, while a third insisted that ASIAN IMMIGRANTS ARE TAKING ALL THE JOBS — LET'S STOP THEM COMING HERE BEFORE THEY TAKE OVER THE COUNTRY.

He had seen two of the posters taped on the window of an empty store. Casey told himself he could check the rest of the stuff in the room later. Right now he had to contact somebody and get help. He turned on the fax. Nothing. Next he tried the computer. Maybe he could email Hank. The computer worked, and he was able to send a message to his brother. According to the machine, his message had been sent but that didn't mean Hank would look at it anytime soon. Who else had an email address he knew by heart? No one else in Richford sprang to mind. He hadn't been here long enough. But what about his grandmother in Regina!

Casey and his grandmother had "talked" from all over the place. But this was Friday. *Da Vinci's Inquest* reruns were on television, and she would be watching the show right now. He sent her a message, anyway.

Grandma, call the police in Richford and tell them to get out to the Old Willson with Two Ls Place right away. Tell them I'm here with Mr. Deverell, my science teacher, and that he's been hit on the head and is unconscious. This isn't a joke. Do it, Grandma, and do it now. Please ... Casey.

Who else could he contact? He wished more than ever that his parents had let him have a cell phone. It would have come in handy right now. Then he remembered the ad for the computer store in the new mall where Hank had won the prize. This time his message was:

This isn't a joke. My name is Casey Templeton. Hank, my brother, won your computer prize. I'm out at the Old Willson with Two Ls Place, using a computer that's here in the attic. Mr. Deverell, the science teacher at Clarence Wilberforce Willson High School in Richford, Alberta, is half frozen, badly hurt, and unconscious. Please contact the police and have them get medical help here right away.

That was all Casey could think of doing. He went back to the living room. The fire was almost out, and though he had left the attic door open, the lower room was no warmer. All he had to put on the fire was a pillow. It ignited slowly, sent more smelly billows of ash into the room, and gradually began to burn. Casey sat against the wall beside Mr. Deverell, gently easing the teacher's battered head onto his lap.

So what was the payoff for the haters? Casey wondered as he closed his eyes and settled his shoulders more comfortably. What was the point of all the crazy stuff they were doing? Were they aiming just to make life miserable for the groups they focused their hate on — Jews, immigrants, gays, old people, and the disabled — or did they want to get rid of them entirely? That was pretty heavy thinking, and Casey tried to get his mind on something else.

Only the occasional sizzle of burning feathers broke the silence in the old house. Casey burrowed deeper into his coat for warmth, but the bare floor was so cold that his backside was getting numb. He leaned over for a pillow and tucked it under him.

At least he could sit in comfort. Casey eased Mr. Deverell's left arm upward, carefully pulled off the stiff glove, and gently rubbed the man's icy hand. When it started to feel a little less cold, Casey did the same thing for the right hand.

His thoughts drifted back to the room with all the hate literature. It must be a kind of "hate cell," a sort of headquarters for racists. There had been a real buzz in Richford when a new family had moved down the street from the Templeton house a few weeks ago. Casey had walked to school with the two children, Laszlo and Anna, both in grade one, though Laszlo was several years older than his sister. The language they spoke had fascinated Casey. His dad had said it was called Romany. The kids' mother, his father had told him, was a Roma or Gypsy who had married Daisy Olberg's kid brother, Jack McKay, when he was doing repairs on a Canadian nuclear reactor in Romania many years ago.

"But Maria wasn't the kind of Gypsy who goes from place to place in a caravan," his father had said. "Daisy tells us Maria was the daughter of a Gypsy orchestra leader in an upscale Bucharest hotel. She sang with the orchestra, and that's where Jack met her. When Jack was killed, the government helped Daisy bring Maria and the children to live in Richford."

Two weeks ago a poster, the HONK IF YOU HATE GYPSIES one, had been found stapled to the gate in front of the Olbergs' place. Someone had heard a horn honking around two in the morning, but nobody had seen the car or had any idea who was doing the honking. And then there was the hit-and-run of Maria McKay.

"Daisy told me," Casey's mother had said to Casey and his dad, "that even before the 'accident,' Maria was finding Richford very limiting and was thinking of moving away. This will make her want to move all the more."

The week before Maria was struck by a car a pipe bomb had gone off at the Finegoods' big clothing and dry goods store. Swastikas were painted on their house's double garage doors, with THE HOLOCAUST IS A HOAX poster taped in the middle of them. The poster had been printed by the National Alliance. Hank had discovered that the National Alliance was the largest and most active neo-Nazi organization in the United States and Canada.

"The Web info says," Hank had quoted to Casey, "that the National Alliance's current strength can be attributed to 'its skillful embrace of technology, its willingness to cooperate with other extremists, its energetic recruitment and other promotional activities, and its vicious propaganda.'"

"I'm telling you, Casey," Marcie Finegood had said as they were going into English class the day after the bombing, "whoever did that to my dad's store better watch out!" Her eyes were red and her eyelids swollen, but her chin was thrust forward. "I'm mad as heck and I'm ready to fight back."

"I'm with you, Marcie," he had said, smiling. "I'm ready to do something radically mean to whoever did this to your family."

He felt good now, knowing his discoveries would be the first step toward finding out who was responsible.

A tremor went through the hand Casey was rubbing — the first sign of life in Mr. Deverell besides a pulse and shallow breathing. Would his messages get through to the Richford police? Casey wondered. What if they didn't? What if he had to spend the night in this cold room? He couldn't keep the fire going much longer, and if Mr. Deverell started to cool down again, that wouldn't be good.

Casey turned off the flashlight to conserve the battery. Was there anything else he could do? He switched on the light again to check his watch — nine-thirty. The two hours he had given himself to get the pipe and return home were up. Not that his parents would be home anytime soon.

He thought he would try a little telepathy. *Grandma, can you hear me? Please open your email and follow instructions. Hank, finish your game and check your email ... check your mail ... check your mail ... Hank, check your email right now!*

Casey waited, then put another pillow on the fire. Even though he was cold, it was hard to stay awake. He went through the telepathy bit another couple of times, but nothing happened. "I'll try it one more time," he whispered to himself, but as he chanted, sleep overcame him. A quick movement of Mr. Deverell's head jerked him awake, though. Why was the room so terribly cold?

"Oh, no!" Casey put Mr. Deverell's head down gently and crawled over to the fireplace. Not a spark! He tried blowing on the smouldering pillow. A cloud of half-burned feathers and ashes flew into his eyes.

Poor Mr. Deverell, he thought, wouldn't last long now. Casey had to get back to town. He just had to.

Tucking the last few pillows tightly around his teacher, Casey picked up the flashlight. It wouldn't go on. He unscrewed the bottom and switched the batteries. It flickered on and off a few times and then went out. Would he dare try getting back to town without the light? He could see the headline in the national edition of Toronto's *Globe and Mail*, which the Templetons had delivered each morning: BOY AND TEACHER VICTIMS OF CENTRAL ALBERTA'S FIRST VICIOUS SNOWSTORM.

Casey shut the door of the Old Willson Place, crossed the porch, and went down the front steps. He ploughed through the deep snow as far as the gate, then trudged down the road to the field. Crossing the frozen field the first time had been hard; re-crossing it now with the snow so deep would be almost impossible.

At least he could tell if he was going straight across. If his progress was too easy, that meant he was moving along a furrow, not over it, so he pushed himself over another snow-piled furrow, then another until he fell. Snow spilled into his boots, and he felt the cold on his bare legs above his socks.

What if he took a tumble and couldn't get up again? He would freeze to death and so would Mr. Deverell.

Casey hauled himself to his feet. A few furrows later he fell again and then again. Each time he sprawled a little longer in the snow. Each time it took more effort to get up until at last he stayed put.

"Get up!" he yelled. "Get going!"

Another voice, inside him, insisted, *I can't. It's so nice and quiet here and I feel so deliciously sleepy. I'll just lie here a little longer.*

"Get up, Casey! Get up!"

Later ... after, he thought. Then he began to dream about beating everyone else in the world at the snowboarding competition in Banff. Eventually, he wasn't dreaming at all. He just lay there, buried in the heavy snow.

CHAPTER THREE

Casey didn't know where he was when he woke and saw the worried faces of his parents and Hank hovering over him. In his freezing sleep he hadn't heard the ambulance siren, hadn't been aware of the frantic calling of his name by his father and Hank, didn't know he had been discovered and carried by his dad to the ambulance parked at the Willson Place where a doctor and two paramedics worked on Mr. Deverell.

"So, Casey," Hank said now, patting his shoulder, "you're some kind of hero saving Mr. Deverell's life. But what the heck were you doing at the Old Willson Place? And why didn't you stay put after you sent the emails?"

"Maybe he shouldn't be talking yet," Casey's mother said, giving her youngest son a look of loving concern.

"Hey, I'm fine," Casey told them. He tried to sit up, felt dizzy, and collapsed against the pillows. "The fire went out and I wasn't sure any of my messages got through, so I thought I'd better get to town for help before Mr. D. froze to death."

Casey's father had been listening in silence. Now he spoke. "That doesn't explain what you were doing out there, Casey. No question you saved Mr. Deverell's life, but going out there alone at night wasn't smart. Feel up to explaining it?"

"May I have a glass of water?" Casey croaked.

His mother poured ice water from a fat green plastic jug on the bedside table into a squat glass with a straw, gently lifted Casey's head, and put another pillow under it, then handed him the glass.

"How's Mr. D.?" Casey asked after he took a long swig.

"Not good," his dad said. "Still unconscious, poor soul. Casey, we're waiting for an explanation."

"Okay, Dad, here it comes." He handed the glass back to his mother. "But don't expect it in point form."

Chief Superintendent Templeton was a stickler for having all reports made to him as: point one, such and such, point two, such and such else, et cetera. Casey just wasn't up to thinking like that. His father nodded, and he began.

"It all started yesterday after gym when I heard Kevin Schreiver and Terry Bracco say they were heading out to the Old Willson Place right after school to —"

"Smoke," interrupted his father.

Casey nodded. He caught a fleeting smile around his dad's eyes. Did his father know that because he had done the same thing once upon a time? "I decided to get there before them and ..."

"And ...?" his mother prompted.

"And be there smoking a pipe when they got there."

"This pipe?" Casey's father took the antique pipe from his pocket, his face now unsmiling.

Casey nodded. "I figured they'd think that was a pretty cool thing to do. And they did. I hardly smoked. The tobacco I got out of Hank's cigarettes tasted awful, but I did get the pipe lit. Anyway, the pipe wasn't in my pocket when I went to put it back in its case at home, so I figured I must have lost it at the Willson Place. That's why I went back — to find it."

"Two Mounties from Fraserville are out in the hall," his father said. "You can tell the rest of your story to all of us together. Hank, will you get Staff Sergeant Deblo and Constable Hexall?"

Casey asked for the glass and took another long sip of water, thinking he would try to give his report to the Mounties in point form. Maybe that would put his dad in a better mood.

"Point one," Casey began, glancing at his dad. "As I looked over at the Old Willson Place when I was crossing the field, I saw a light for a few seconds in the front window. It moved, went out, and didn't come on again."

"Deverell?" Staff Sergeant Deblo questioned.

"I don't think so, sir," Casey said. "I found him about twenty minutes later. Can't see how he could've been that stiff and cold and snow-covered in such a short time. And I didn't see any light nearby when I found him."

Deblo frowned. "And our searchers didn't find a light near the gate. But Deverell would have needed a light, so where did it go? And how did he get to the Willson Place? Surely, he drove the back road we took and wouldn't have walked across the field the way you did, Casey. We've checked. His car was in his garage, but it had been driven sometime after the snow started. There were still wet areas under the tires."

"I didn't see a car or any tire tracks out there," Casey said." "But it was snowing pretty hard by the time I found him. The tracks would have been covered up."

The police had Casey tell how he had moved Mr. Deverell into the house. When he was finished, his dad said, "Casey, I'm very proud of your problem-solving ability."

Compliments from his father were few and far between, and this was one Casey knew he would treasure forever.

When Casey got to point eleven — his discovery of the "hate" headquarters — and explained about sending the emails, it was Staff Sergeant Deblo's turn to praise him. "You should consider the Mounties as a career, Casey. Your kind of thinking would be a real asset to the force."

After the Mounties finished questioning Casey, they politely said no to his suggestion that he help in the investigation. The focus of their inquiries, they told him, would, of course, be: Who was responsible for the violence against Mr. Deverell, the Finegoods, and the Olbergs? Who had set up the Hate Cell? And who owned the computer equipment?

Casey had those questions and so many other things to ponder that he told himself he didn't really mind all the snow-shovelling he would have to do as punishment for his reckless behaviour. Maybe the Mounties could get along without him, but he bet there was still something he knew that they didn't.

When he did return from the hospital, Casey not only had to shovel his own driveway and long sidewalk but the sidewalk of the Masons' house next door and the Olbergs' place next to it. That meant he was shovelling a whole city block every time it snowed, and it did so every day during his first week home. Worse, he was going to have to shovel like that all winter — and for no pay. Chief Superintendent Templeton believed in meting out punishment that "made the perpetrator think a lot about what he had done and kept him fit, as well."

Now, in the midst of his latest shovelling chore, the two little McKay kids came out with an invitation from Mrs. Olberg to join them for a cup of hot cocoa when he finished. Laszlo and Anna went back to tell their aunt that Casey would love some cocoa, and Laszlo returned with a shovel to help Casey so he could finish sooner.

Mrs. Olberg — Daisy — was an old friend of Casey's parents. It was she the Templetons had asked to search for a house for them when they knew they would soon be moving back to Richford. That it was almost next door to her was a plus for everybody.

Casey took off his shovelling clothes in the Olbergs' back hall and came up the few steps into the kitchen.

"Boy, your dad's a tough customer, Casey," Mrs. Olberg said, pouring Casey a big mug of hot cocoa and putting two homemade doughnuts on a plate in front of him. "I hear you're elected to shovel our whole block all this winter. Pretty nice for the rest of us, but poor you. Laszlo wants to help, so let him."

"I will," Casey said. "But, Mrs. O., we're getting so much snow so darn early this year. Shovelling's all I seem to do. I hardly have time for anything else."

Casey heard someone walking down the stairs. When he looked up, he saw Laszlo's mother enter the kitchen. He had met her before, of course, but was just as impressed each time. Maria McKay was very beautiful, with flashing black eyes and long black hair done in a thick braid that hung over her right shoulder. She wore a silver-blue tailored blouse and an ankle-length skirt of flowing cornflower-blue silk. Her neck was encased in a wide brace, and she limped a little.

Casey stood. "Good afternoon, Mrs. McKay."

"Hello, Casey," she said. "Sit down for goodness' sake." Her English was very good. Just the odd word sounded foreign.

"Would you like some cocoa, Maria?" Mrs. Olberg asked. "Or tea? I can make some in a minute and I'd like a cup, too."

"Tea would be good. Thank you, Daisy." Laszlo's mother turned to Casey. "Tell me what's happening with the investigation of the idiots who nearly killed me. Is it known yet who's responsible?"

Casey took a gulp of cocoa. "Well, I'm not officially in on the investigation, of course, but I can tell you the team has some promising leads."

"What you're really saying is nobody knows much."

"Maybe not, but I'll tell you this. My dad knows an awful lot about what makes these 'hate' types tick, and you better believe he'll have some answers soon."

Mrs. McKay sighed. "That's what Daisy keeps telling me, but I don't know. I really thought coming to Canada would be the most wonderful thing for my children. I thought they would grow up in a land free of hate. I can't believe how wrong I was. Gypsies have a hard time of it everywhere in Europe. Look what's happened in the Czech Republic — people building a fence between themselves and Gypsy neighbours. You come to expect things like that in the Old Country. But here? Why here?"

Casey didn't know what to say, but he felt he had to answer, anyway. "Well, Mrs. McKay, there are probably only a few of these haters around at most."

Mrs. McKay took the cup of tea from her sister-in-law and shook her head. "I wish I could believe that, Casey, but every time I go downtown in Richford I get a lot of mean comments said to me. I swear there's a lot of hate in those voices."

"What's in those voices," Casey said with wisdom beyond his fourteen years, "is envy. Pure green-eyed envy!"

Mrs. McKay pushed another doughnut onto Casey's plate. "What a nice thing for you to say."

"Thanks, but I've had too much already," Casey said. "And, Mrs. McKay, I'm sure you'll soon feel better about living here." He stood to go, then turned to Laszlo. "I've got a lot of my old books around, Laszlo. You can borrow any of them for as long as you like."

"Can I get some now?" Laszlo asked.

"Sure, come on." Casey opened the back door and glanced out. "On second thought, Laszlo, come tomorrow instead, right after school." It was snowing once more. He was going to have to push the shovel around yet again.

Back outside in the falling snow, Casey let his mind dwell on the situation at his new school as he shovelled. *Now that the guys have asked me to join the Coyote Club at school, and Marcie Finegood has smiled at me three times, I'm really in. If it'll just stop snowing so I can take advantage of the situation, I'll be set.*

When Casey finally finished shovelling and returned home, there was nobody else there. He set the table, scooped six ginger cookies out of the cookie jar, put three back as he remembered the two doughnuts he had eaten at the Olbergs', poured himself a glass of milk, and headed for his room. At his desk he took out a notebook and turned to a page where numbered questions and answers were set up in point form:

Question 1: Was Mr. Deverell part of what was going on in the attic of the Willson Place, or was he on the trail of whoever had set up the Hate Cell?

Answer 1: Mr. D. never said anything political in class. But a science teacher didn't have the same opportunities to brainwash kids as a social studies teacher did. Mom's friend, Hilda Deverell (Mr. D.'s recent ex — his first wife died years ago), said he was a very tolerant person but a very nosy one. She could see him spying, but not being part of a hate group.

Question 2: Who drove Mr. D.'s car back to his garage?

Answer 2: It had to be someone who: (a) knew where he lived and that he lived alone; (b) didn't expect Mr. D. to be found so soon; and (c) counted on a search beginning only after Mr. D. failed to show up to teach the next day.

Casey figured Answer 2(a) could be anyone in Richford over the age of ten. Sitting back, he ate a cookie, then resumed his work. He wrote all he had learned from listening to conversations his dad had had with the RCMP in the Templetons' living room during the past few nights. The Mounties, knowing of Casey's father's experience in Bosnia, much of it dealing with ethnic cleansing and racial hatred, had asked him to co-direct the investigative team. Standing on a basement chair, Casey had positioned himself under a wooden grille built into the living-room floor and listened to his father and the Mounties talk. Later he had written down what he had discovered. Now he reread his notes:

- The computer, printer, scanner, and fax found in the Willson attic had been bought for cash in Markham, Ontario, a year before, along with a three-year service agreement signed by an Elsie Tavich.
- The computer had been repaired at Apple Service in Fraserville six months ago and had been signed for by Elsie Tavich (though the signature differed from the one on the service agreement).
- An Apple Service clerk remembered carrying the computer into the store from a new red Toyota pickup because the woman who drove the truck had a splint on her right hand and she had signed awkwardly with her left hand.

- A police artist's sketch of Elsie Tavich had been prepared with the help of the clerk. Staff in the Markham store confirmed it was the woman they had sold the machines to — she had been in the store often before she settled on the "package."
- All owners of new red Toyota pickups, some thirty in and around Fraserville, were questioned, but none were proven to have been near the Apple store on the date in question.
- The hate posters had been printed in Idaho. Similar posters had been discovered in two Ontario cities, Toronto and Hamilton, and also in the South Okanagan in British Columbia. There was no way to trace how or when they had arrived in Richford.

Casey ate the last cookie, pushed his chair back, and put his feet on the desk. He thought about how the investigation was developing so far. His father and Hank, who knew more about computers than anyone in town and who had been hired by the police to assist in this particular case, had spent a lot of time in the Willson attic.

"You look like you're doing some pretty deep thinking, bro'," Hank said, breaking into Casey's reverie.

Casey looked up. "I thought you weren't coming home for supper."

"I'm not. I'm just here to check something on my computer."

Casey rubbed his chin. "Hank, I've been thinking ..."

His brother grinned. "Tell me something new."

"I know all about the posters and stuff in the Willson attic, but what else was up there? Can you tell me?"

"I guess it'd be okay. Come to my room."

Casey got up and followed Hank to his bedroom. His brother took a seat at the computer, and Casey pulled up a chair next to him.

"Whoever was using that computer in the attic," Hank said, "bookmarked a number of sites. I downloaded files from a bunch of white supremacist and Holocaust-denial groups, including the National Alliance, the National Socialist Movement of Illinois, the Heritage Front, Skin-Net, the European Christian Defence League, and on and on. I also found out that the area Internet provider of all these is a technology centre in Idaho."

"What's the worst thing you found up there besides what's in the computer?"

"That's easy to answer — *The Turner Diaries*. A well-worn, heavily underlined copy."

"Hey," Casey said, "that's what those Oklahoma City bombing guys had."

"Yeah, it details a successful world revolution by an all-white army and the systematic extermination of blacks, Jews, and other minorities."

"Could that ever happen?"

"The diaries say it could — and should," Hank said. "And look at these." He handed Casey a sheaf of papers. "These are transcripts of radio broadcasts by the book's author, Andrew Macdonald, who was really William Luther Pierce, head of the National Alliance. He died in 2002, but his teachings are still widely followed. Between the book and these transcripts you can find out how to commit every kind of destruction. These guys use very sophisticated hate sites to showcase their racist and neo-Nazi ideas. They disrupt chat rooms and send thousands of unsolicited emails full of their views. And here's where they really do a lot of damage. They use Internet forums as a low-cost, convenient recruitment tool."

Hank had found lots of emails addressed to "White Canada." The server's post office box was under the name R.U. Withus.

"The Mounties have a watch on the post office box," Hank said, "but there's been no activity since the night of the attack on Mr. Deverell.

Poor Mr. D., Casey thought, he was still totally out of it.

"I gotta go, bro," Hank said, slipping a memory stick into his pocket. "See you later."

Alone again and frustrated at not being able to help in the investigation, Casey reviewed everything he knew so far carefully. Then he thought about the scraps of paper he had used to light the fire in the Willson place. Had anything been written on them? He couldn't recall.

He did remember thinking when he first saw the long, thin brass screws going through the crossed boards that they weren't the type a person could find just anywhere. For their science project he and Bryan had talked to the people at Sanford's Hardware on Main Street in Richford. Mr. Sanford himself had brought out a catalogue and ordered the screws from it. Casey and Bryan had needed only six of the minimum order of a dozen. Maybe the other six had been sold locally. Perhaps the ones in the door were those very screws. If they were, it would mean two things: the screws had been put in the door recently, and someone at the hardware store might recall who had bought them. He wondered what excuse he could use to ask the staff at Sanford's.

Casey closed his eyes and focused on the night at the Willson house. Step by step he pictured everything that had happened: Mr. Deverell lying in the snow, his hunt for something to pull him on — the drapes! No one on the investigation team had seen them because Casey had burned them. But he had known when he pulled them open the afternoon of the attack that they had been new. And he could remember the pattern clearly. If he couldn't trace the long brass screws, he might be able to find out who had bought the drapes and where. They would have been especially made for the Willson front window, he figured, because it was an odd shape — wide but not very high. He was pretty sure Richford didn't have a store that made drapes.

"Come to supper, Casey. Now!"

Casey figured his dad's loud, deep voice could be heard all over town.

"Coming!" he shouted, wishing Hank was eating at home for a change so his parents wouldn't have just him to concentrate on. He put away his notebook, feeling pretty upbeat. At least he had a couple of ideas he could explore on his own.

CHAPTER FOUR

As they settled down to eat, Casey said to his mother, "I hate the drapes in my room. They must have been some girl's. I'd like to choose my own."

"I wondered," his mother said, "how long you'd put up with them. We'll be going into Fraserville on Saturday. Why don't you come and choose your pattern at Vance's Draperies? I'll put the ones you have now in the new guest room — when Dad finally finishes it."

Casey's grandmother was coming for a visit as soon as the guest room was done, and Casey figured that might have something to do with how long his father was taking on the job.

"Why not get them at Thrift Mart right here in

Richford?" his dad asked. "Vance's will be expensive."

"Not necessarily," Mrs. Templeton said. "Casey has a corner window that'll be tricky finding ready-made drapes to fit, and Vance's is having a huge sale. We'll come off just fine. And speaking of the guest room, Colin, I got a note from Mother today. She's planning her Christmas itinerary and wants to visit us for New Year's."

"Oh ..." Casey's father didn't look happy.

"Why not get Casey to give you a hand with the guest room?" his mother suggested. "You'd like to help your dad, wouldn't you, Casey?"

"Well ... sure," Casey said slowly. "What would I be doing?"

"Mainly be a gofer and keep me company once in a while," his dad said. "I'd be grateful. I hate working down there alone."

This was a side of his father Casey had never seen. "Well, sure, Dad. I'll keep you company when I can. I'll be free tonight after supper. I don't have any homework that has to be done by tomorrow."

His father beamed, genuinely happy. "That'll be great. We can survey the situation."

Casey caught his mother smiling to herself. Then his mind returned to the puzzle of who had bought the new drapes for the Willson Place. In just two days he would have his answer. He could see the write-up in all the newspapers:

Knightly Charles Templeton, known to all as Casey, gave the Royal Canadian Mounted

Police vital information they needed to track down the attackers of Mr. Semple Deverell, science teacher at the Clarence Wilberforce Willson High School in Richford, Alberta, at the headquarters of the hate ring just outside the town. Casey's contribution was the name of the person who had recently purchased drapes for the lower front windows of the Old Willson Place where the sophisticated apparatus and headquarters of the hate organization were discovered.

"Your mother has asked you three times now, Casey, if you'd like more lasagna," his father was saying. "Come down to Earth and answer."

"Sorry, Mom," Casey said. "Yes, I'd like a lot more lasagna, please."

An hour later Casey and his dad were on the lower level, studying the roughed-in guest room and adjoining bath. The Templeton house was a classic forty-year-old split level — it actually had five levels, including a small one over the back patio, which had beds for Jake and Billy when they came for holidays. The room he and his dad were now examining had the makings of a perfect guest room with its own entrance from the patio. Casey looked around. One day he planned to have this room, so it wasn't a bad idea to have some input into how it was completed.

"One thing I'm going to do," his father told him, "is soundproof this room."

"Sounds good, but with Grandma down here we should have a way of hearing her if she needs help."

"We can rig up something, but we've got to keep the noise of her television, radio, and stereo down for the rest of us."

Casey nodded. "Yeah, I remember the last time she stayed with us she had one of the regular bedrooms and we could hear everything. And she played those CDs of hers so loud!"

"Exactly. It was one of the few times I was home in a year, and I couldn't get a decent night's sleep."

"You like Grandma, though, don't you?"

"I love her. She's got the same strong character your mother has, but she likes her gadgets, brings what she wants, like her laptop, and wants things her way. This room will be perfect ... if we ever get it done."

They were each sitting on a sawhorse, and Casey watched as his father gazed at the room. "Dad, are you glad to be retired?" It had never occurred to him before that his father might not be happy. Heavy silence filled the unfinished room. It went on so long that Casey wondered if his dad had heard his question.

"I guess I am, Casey. I've been telling myself for years it's what I wanted to do. But my life's been action-oriented for so long that it's hard to slow down so completely. You know your mom and I always planned to come back to Richford, but honestly, Casey ..."

"Is it this hate business that's put you off?"

"Well, partly. I'm disappointed with what's going on in town but, on the other hand, I'm grateful to be involved in the investigation." His father thought for a moment, then added, "But when that's over, then what? I mean, I've got this room to do, and now that you're going to give me a hand, I think I'll feel more like getting it done, but again, then what? I've got to find something else to do."

"Does Mom know how you feel?"

"Sure. She says we don't have to stay here if I can't find something worthwhile to do, not just something that's busywork. You see, Casey, all those years on the force I never took time for any hobbies. I've thought some about writing my memoirs, but I know I never will. I honestly don't know ..." Again silence filled the room.

A change of subject was called for. "Hey, Dad, what if we put in a whirlpool tub? Grandma would love that."

"She sure would. We all would. I was thinking of just a shower, but there's no reason why the bathroom can't be bigger. We'll just move the studs over a half metre or so."

"And, Dad, why couldn't we use the other half of this level for an exercise room? Heck, we could even put one of those pools in the basement. You know, the kind where you swim against some jets."

Chief Inspector Templeton chuckled. "No pool unless we win a lottery, Casey, but I can see the gym. Let's go up and tell your mother our new plans." He put his arm around Casey's shoulders as they climbed the wide steps to the main level.

X X X

"I'll come by in about an hour, Casey," his mother said as she parked outside Vance's Draperies that Saturday. "If you decide on a pattern before that and go somewhere else, just be sure you're back here by then."

"Sure, Mom."

Casey had never imagined there could be so many kinds and patterns of drapery fabrics. When a clerk asked him if there were something special he was looking for, he said, "The pattern I want has small light blue and red circles on a very dark blue background."

"Offhand I can't picture the pattern you described," said the clerk, a slim young woman with long brown hair in a ponytail, big brown eyes, and a wide smile. Casey figured she was about eighteen or so. "Can you tell me what sort of fabric you want?"

"Pretty heavy," Casey said, recalling the beating the drapes at the Old Willson Place had taken.

"That doesn't tell me much. Sit at this table and I'll bring you some sample books to go through." In a matter of minutes the pile of sample books the clerk brought to Casey's table got very high and wide. "Just come and get me if you want more books, or if you find what you're looking for." She went off to serve another customer.

Casey hung his coat on the back of a chair, put his baseball hat on the table beside him, and started flipping over sample after sample. There were lots of patterns he could imagine in his own room, and to make his search appear legitimate he marked several with yellow Post-its the clerk had given him, but he found nothing like the pattern he was hunting for.

When the clerk brought a new batch of books, she stopped and stared at him. "You're what's-his-name from Richford, the boy who saved the teacher's life. I know you from the picture in the *Fraserville Herald*. I didn't recognize you with your hat on, but you're so blond you're hard to miss."

Casey didn't know whether to be pleased or not. Once people saw how blond he was they usually remembered him. "Yes, I'm Casey Templeton."

"Casey! That's it! Nice to meet you, Casey. I'm Sarah Vance. My dad owns this place. Do you know anything new about the case? I've been following every news story for a paper I'm writing for my sociology class."

"Well, the Mounties don't share their secrets with me but —" Casey stopped. It dawned on him that Sarah could really help. Being related to the owner of the drapery store meant she could get access to the files and find out who had bought the fabric, or if indeed it had come from Vance's. "Would helping to solve the case be a plus for your paper?"

"Are you kidding? I'd get a top mark for sure. Help how?"

Casey hadn't quite finished telling Sarah when he felt a hand on his shoulder.

"Still at it, Casey?" his mother asked as Sarah moved away. "Show me what you found that you like." She sat down, and Casey passed her the books he had tagged. "That one's out. Even on sale it would cost too much. All the ones in this book are too expensive." She searched through several other sample books, then called Sarah over. Casey introduced the clerk to his mother. "Your sale ad mentioned discontinued lines, Sarah. Could you show us what you have?"

There was something about the easy way Sarah smiled at people as she carried the big books between counters stacked high with coloured and patterned fabric that made Casey feel he had known her before. In their brief talk he had discovered she was bright, caring, and comfortable to be with. She was like … she was like Hank's Cindy! Not in looks. Sarah wasn't tall like Cindy, and Sarah's brown hair was slicked back not flyaway gold, but they both had that wonderful way of making a person feel good. Casey made up his mind. Before this hate business was wound up he was going to see that Hank met Sarah.

"These are patterns the manufacturers have only limited supplies of," Sarah said as she handed Casey's mother a thick folder. "And, of course, we have a shelf of remnants — some with really good sizes and prices."

"You have a look at the remnants, Casey," his mother said. "I'll go through this folder."

Five minutes into the exploration of remnants Casey spotted a thin roll of the heavy navy blue fabric with small red and light blue circles and beckoned to Sarah. "This is it! Is there any way you can get the names of the people who ordered it since it's been in your dad's store?"

Sarah nodded. "I'm pretty sure I can, but it'll take a while. I'm just helping out during university reading week. Dad scheduled the sale for when I'd be home. I go back Monday and won't have time to do any checking before that. But I do plan to be here next weekend, so I'll do it then. For now I'll put it out of sight." She picked up the slim roll of fabric. "I'll give you my cell phone number. Call me a week from tomorrow." She wrote the number on a yellow Post-it and handed it to Casey.

"Any luck, Casey?" Mrs. Templeton asked, giving Sarah back the folder. "I didn't find anything."

"Let's just forget it, Mom." Casey had found out what he wanted to know and was now eager to get out of the store.

"Tell me," his mother asked Sarah thoughtfully, "does Vance's dye drapes?"

"Some fabrics dye beautifully, others, not," Sarah said. "It costs quite a bit because the lining and the draperies have to be dyed separately, but of course it's a lot cheaper than almost any new ones would be."

"I may bring some into you in a week or so," Mrs. Templeton told Sarah. As they left the store, she said to Casey, "If you don't mind having drapes that are dyed, we could buy the TV you've been wanting for your bedroom with what we'd save."

"Terrific," Casey said.

He smiled to himself. Now wouldn't that be a nice bonus? Solve the Deverell mystery, have Hank and Sarah meet, be a hero, and get a television, too. He was sure that with Sarah's help he would find out who had ordered the drapes for the big front window at the Old Willson Place. And once he knew that he could ... well, Casey wasn't too sure what he could do. He would figure that out when the time came.

CHAPTER FIVE

It was as he was leaving the skating shack the next Friday night, feeling pretty pleased because Marcie Finegood had skated more with him than with any of the other guys and not so pleased because Marcie's dad had come to pick her up early, that Casey heard his name being called in a raspy whisper.

"Casey! Over here, Casey!"

He looked around. At the corner of the skating shack, just past the circle of the outdoor light, someone was beckoning. No one else was around. Casey walked over. "Bryan?" he said, recognizing his hailer. "What gives?"

"Casey, I've *got* to talk to someone."

"Well, sure, but let's go inside. It's too cold out here."

"No, come to my place. My folks are out."

"Okay," Casey agreed. *His* folks were very much *in*. They were having their two-table bridge club tonight, and Casey would rather be just about anywhere else other than home. "So what's up?" he asked Bryan as they walked.

"I've got myself into something pretty bad. Really bad. And I don't now how to get out of it."

"Can't your folks help?"

They turned into the Ogilvys' driveway. Casey had never been in Bryan's house. *But who had been?* Probably nobody at school. It was a nice-looking place — a three-storey pale blue colonial with white pillars, trim, and shutters. It seemed to Casey like a paint company's television advertisement.

"They'd kill me if they knew," Bryan told him, opening the front door to a large hall with polished dark oak floors, an oriental carpet, and huge Chinese vases.

Casey searched for a place to put his skates. He was afraid they might drip on the floor, so he put his coat down and the skates on top of it.

"Honest, Casey, I don't know why I did it."

"Well, tell me what it's all about." Casey followed Bryan up a carpeted staircase, along a hall, and into a huge bedroom. "Wow!" He stared at a computer setup that blew Hank's out of the water. "Is there anything you don't have?"

Bryan sat on his computer chair and sagged. "Not much."

"So *tell* me." Casey sat opposite his friend. "Start at the beginning and tell me what's going on."

"Okay, you're new here and we're friends if not buddies, but you've seen how all the other kids and even the teachers treat me. The only teacher who ever showed any interest in me was Mr. Deverell. If he dies ... oh, Casey, if he dies I'll be partly responsible. I've just got to have someone understand why I did what I did and maybe help bail me out. And I've got to try to make up for it."

Bryan clenched his fists and closed his eyes for a moment. "Anyway, I've never been asked to be a part of any group or club at school. I don't know what it is about me that puts people off. More than one thing, I guess. We're never here for the summers or for any of the holidays, and my parents ... well, they're different from other people's. And I never know what to say to get people to like me."

"You seem to be able to talk to me."

"That's because right away *you* talked to *me*. You're the first kid to take any notice of me in years. Anyway, I never feel part of things."

"What about your family?" Casey glanced around the beautifully furnished room. "You're part of your family, and they obviously care a lot about you."

"You think so? My parents were married ten years before they had me, and they still really only care about each other. They can afford it, so they buy me anything I want just to keep me out of the way."

"Really?" Casey thought how his parents got along great with each other but still always concerned themselves about their sons.

"Well, as you said, I've got a great computer. It's about my fifth, and I've been exploring the Web for years. There are three chat rooms I really like, and I have real *friends* in them from all over the world. You know what I mean by chat rooms?"

"Of course I know," Casey said. "My brother, Hank, has a great time arguing with people in his groups."

"Well, about a year ago one of the chat rooms started getting messages from an outside group suggesting we get in touch with them for exciting new conversations and ideas. I resisted for ages, but they kept on and on about what we were missing, what did we have to lose, and that once we contacted them we'd be in with technologically elite kindred spirits."

"So you went for it?"

Bryan sighed. "About eight months ago I contacted the website they said to and made the awful mistake of giving them not only my real name and email but even my home address."

"Oh, boy!" Casey shook his head. Hank had always told him how careful you had to be on the Internet.

"At first it was pretty exciting, and I felt I finally belonged to an easy bunch to talk to. A lot of their messages were based on Bible teachings and were written so powerfully that I got caught up in it all. And then ... then ..."

"Then what?" Casey pressed.

"Then they asked me to distribute some anti-gay pamphlets. They said it would establish me as a real worker for the cause."

Casey could hardly believe his ears. "You're the one who delivered all those pamphlets last month? You must have spent the whole night at it!"

Bryan seemed ashamed. "I did. And after that they sent me some drugs."

"Drugs?"

"So I'd feel obliged to them, I guess," Bryan explained. "I hid the parcel in here." He walked over to a tall cupboard, opened the bottom doors, pulled out a stack of books, and showed Casey a small, tightly sealed package.

"How did you know what was in the package?" Casey asked. "It's sealed shut."

"Oh, I resealed it very carefully. It's got pills in it stamped with butterflies. That's how Ecstasy's sometimes marked. I found that out on the Internet. I had the package for about a week and was going to send it back when I got an email that said if I didn't do what they wanted next they'd tell my parents I was on drugs."

"Why didn't you just throw the package out and stop emailing them? And besides, they still could be any kind of pills and not something illegal."

Bryan looked miserable. "Sure, I suppose they could be something harmless, but how do I know for sure? And I can't ask anyone who might know. As for throwing the whole thing out, I thought of doing that, but the group said if I did that they could still let the police know I got the package and what was in it."

"So what did this group want you to do?" Casey asked.

"Steal some money and send it to them."

"You didn't do that, did you?"

"They said they'd tell my parents if I didn't."

"So you stole money? From who?"

"No, I didn't steal it. I sent them my own money."

"How much?"

Bryan looked at the floor sheepishly. "Four hundred dollars. They think I did steal it, and now they're saying that if I don't keep doing what they order me to do, they'll tell the police."

"Bryan, you can just tell the police they're lying."

"Yeah, but what if the group tells the police about the pamphlets and the drugs and the other stuff?"

"What other stuff?"

Before Bryan could answer they heard the front door open and close.

"My parents!" Bryan cried.

"They'll have seen my skates and coat in the front hall, so they know someone's here," Casey said. "Take me down and introduce me."

"But they'll think it's strange. I never have anybody over."

"Well, you have now." Casey headed out of the room. "How about you come over to my place sometime tomorrow afternoon and you can finish telling me about all this?"

"Thanks, Casey," Bryan said softly.

They were at the bottom of the stairs now, and Bryan's parents were coming out of the living room.

"Mother, Father, this is Casey Templeton."

Mrs. Ogilvy smiled. "Hello, Casey." She was a very pretty, beautifully dressed woman about his mother's age, Casey figured. "You're a friend of Bryan's?" She might as well have said, "But Bryan doesn't have any friends."

Casey grinned. "Yes, ma'am, I am. I was just asking Bryan to come over to our house tomorrow afternoon."

"Templeton, Templeton ..." Mr. Ogilvy, a tall, thin, sandy sort of man in a formal navy blue suit, appraised Casey thoughtfully. "Your father's that army type who's moved back here, right?"

"He's a retired RCMP chief superintendent," Casey said, taking an instant dislike to Bryan's father.

"Ah, yes ..." Mr. Ogilvy turned back into the living room with Bryan's mother at his side.

Bryan shook his head glumly at his parents' rudeness.

"Well, bye, Bryan," Casey said. "See you tomorrow?"

"Thanks again, Casey. I'll come about three if that's okay?" He opened the front door.

"Sure." Casey handed his skates to Bryan as he put on his coat. "Three it is."

He heard the door shut behind him and inhaled some fresh cold air. *My gosh,* he thought, glancing back at the house, *no wonder Bryan doesn't want to tell his parents about all the weird stuff he's into!*

X X X

Casey hung up his coat and skates in the back hall of his house when he returned home from Bryan's place. The smell of fresh coffee and hot cinnamon buns drifting from the kitchen filled his nose, while the sounds of a heated discussion blasting from the living room assaulted his ears. Wow! They were really going on about something — eight people seemed to be talking at once. As Casey strained to catch the drift of the argument, his mother came into the kitchen.

"What's everybody so pumped up about, Mom?" he asked, crossing to take a bun off the hot tray on the kitchen counter as his mother poured coffee from a tall aluminum machine into a serving pot.

"Oh, hi, Casey! Jim Bailey's playing devil's advocate."

"What's devil's advocate mean?"

"It means defending something you don't necessarily believe to get people to argue against you. Jim's taking the side of the people in the area who don't want new people moving in. Here, give me a hand passing around these buns while I freshen up everybody's coffee."

Casey took the plate of buns and followed his mother into the living room.

Daisy Olberg waved at him. "Hello, Casey.

Head this way with the best cinnamon buns on the continent."

Casey passed around the buns, then sat quietly on a footstool in the corner. Trying to think through what Bryan had told him, he found he couldn't help tuning in and out of the debate. Then he caught someone saying, "Newcomers bring in fresh ideas and new blood to an area."

"Maybe so," Jim Bailey answered, "but Grandma Jacobson said to me, 'You take that Pakistani family with the fast-food place on Main Street. They're Muslim. Now, Jim, this area was settled by Lutheran Scandinavians. It's been European and Christian over a hundred years. I say the newcomers should respect that fact, and if they want to live here, they should change their religion and become Christians.'"

Casey watched as Daisy's face got redder and redder. If she didn't get a chance to speak soon, she was going to rupture something.

"If you follow that logic," Daisy finally burst in, "then we Christian Europeans should have adopted the religion of the First Nations who were here a lot longer than a hundred years. Heck, follow Grandma Jacobson's thinking and we should be doing their rain dances."

Jim weighed in again. "Grandma Jacobson speaks for an awful lot of the folks here who say, 'Don't mess with our values and customs.'"

How come everybody sounded right? Casey wondered.

"But times have changed," Casey heard Bill Sanford of Sanford's Hardware point out. "Maybe too much in some ways, but this worry about newcomers eroding our national identity is nuts. We are what we are because of the fantastic mix of peoples."

Who could argue with that? Casey asked himself.

Jim could. "The only place around here that has your fantastic mix, Bill, is Minetown. It's cosmopolitan because of all the miners from everywhere who settled there in the 1920s. Around here there's not much of a mix. People here are traditionally against immigration, which they figure takes jobs away from those who think *they* should have them."

"Just because their families have lived and worked here doesn't mean they can keep others out," Bill said. "The law says anyone can move, live, and work anywhere."

"But," Jim insisted, "folks around here worry that different kinds of people moving in will mean more crime and tension."

Boy, Casey thought, Jim was really on his soapbox. Casey wondered how much of what Jim said was what he believed. Then someone asked, "Why do people think the current immigrants are worse than their own ancestors who came in the past?"

"I think," Casey's mother broke in for the first time as she made the rounds with more coffee, "this anti-immigrant business is racism pure and simple. And it's leading to all the name-calling, harassment, and violence."

Casey was thinking of Maria McKay's "accident" when someone asked his father, "You figure there's a tie-in between what we've been talking about and the establishment of the Hate Cell?"

"Sure," Casey's dad said. "People might say they'd never get involved in hate activities, but the anti-immigration, even racist, attitude of the region makes it an ideal place for spreading white supremacy propaganda."

"Do you think it's somebody from around here who set up the Hate Cell at the Willson Place?" Casey asked.

"It has to be someone who knew about the abandoned Willson Place, Casey. And someone who knows that many people want to keep things as they are."

Casey was wishing Bryan could hear all this when his mother said, "I heard somebody we all know pretty well say she thought it was a terrible waste of taxpayers' money to have brought Jack McKay's widow and kids over from Romania and that while knocking down Maria wasn't right, she wasn't badly hurt."

"Not badly hurt!" Daisy shouted. "She'll be in that neck brace for a long time, and her hip gives her terrible pain."

"And I've heard more than one person," Casey's mother continued, "say Mr. Finegood is sucking the town dry expanding his store like he's done and why doesn't he just take his family and move away and leave the merchandising to people who belong here."

Daisy shook her head angrily. "That's so totally unfair! Mel Finegood is just about the most generous man in the community. What with paying for the new skating shack and having that free kids' skate exchange, not to mention paying for the computers in the schools and the library ..."

Sarah would want to know about this stuff, Casey thought. He reached behind him for a pen and a piece of paper and started to make notes. With what people were saying here and what he was hearing from Bryan, he could give Sarah some interesting information. He also knew Bryan was going to have to talk to his dad tomorrow.

At that moment Casey's father sighed. "In Bosnia I saw where this kind of thinking can lead, but there they had a thousand-year buildup of racial hate."

"I swear it wasn't like this when we left Richford twenty-five years ago," Casey's mother added.

"Sure it was," Daisy said. "It was always there just under the surface."

"Well, what was hidden is really coming out," Katie Sanford, Bill's wife, said. "We had that Ku Klux Klan cross burning a few years ago not all that far away. Word is there's more than one branch of the KKK in this area."

"And remember that trial back in the 1980s of the social studies teacher who brainwashed his classes that the Holocaust was a fraud?" Fred Klatt asked. "A lot of folks believed him, especially many of the kids he preached to."

"That teacher never talked to the soldiers who liberated the concentration camps in the Second World War," Casey's father said, frowning. "I have, and I'm telling you their stories are blood-chilling."

"The brainwashing that teacher did was awful," Bill said, "but what about the stuff being taught in some private schools around here right now? They even ask children the question: 'The Jewish leaders were children of their father the devil — true or false?' And the right answer for them is true."

"There was anti-Jewish feeling around here long before the Holocaust," Jim said, abandoning his devil's advocate role. "In the 1930s when times were really tough, some people in the Alberta government made the Jews the scapegoat for everything that was wrong economically."

"The poor Finegoods," Casey's mother said. "They're the only Jewish family in this area and they're bearing the brunt of all the new anti-Semitic propaganda these Hate Cells are spreading."

"And speaking of the Hate Cell here," said Katie Sanford, who helped out in the school library, "I hear quite a few kids saying if Mr. Deverell had minded his own business he wouldn't have gotten hurt. You can bet they're hearing that at home."

Casey had heard that kind of talk, too.

"Mr. Deverell's as likely to die as get well," Bill Sanford said as he reached for another cinnamon bun. "Can't these people see where this kind of thinking leads? Who will be next?"

"Seems this Hate Cell is part of a newly formed

satellite operation with its home base in Idaho," Casey's father said thoughtfully. "Their white supremacy ideology, like their racist ideology, is a cancer, and as it grows, it'll gain power and influence. At that point anyone who disagrees with them becomes a potential target."

"What I don't get, Dad," Casey said, "is the difference between white supremacy and racism."

"White supremacists concentrate on manipulating white people's fears of being taken over by people who aren't white, then they try to incite those people to take action, which usually results in violence," Casey's dad explained. "Racists generally hate specific races or ethnic groups not necessarily because of their colour or their religion. Sometimes it's just based on ancient prejudices."

"How do racists operate?" Casey asked.

"Sometimes it's subtle, like finding ways to prevent them from renting certain properties. Sometimes it's overt, like destroying their property or encouraging their kids to make fun of minorities. Before the kids around here get whipped up by hate propaganda, we've got to find out who's behind this Hate Cell and flush them out."

"Hear! Hear!" several people called out.

"I'm telling you," Casey's dad continued, "this is such a good town that we should insist on zero tolerance for intolerance."

Jim Bailey laughed. "Spoken like a candidate for something. Whatever you're running for, you've got my vote."

The group decided to pack it in for the evening after that, and when they were gone, Casey and his dad began clearing up.

"You've done enough, Mary," his dad said. "Casey and I will take it from here."

Casey's mother nodded wearily. "Thanks, guys. "I'm really bushed."

"Dad?" Casey asked as he loaded cups and saucers into the dishwasher. "Do you know Mr. Ogilvy?"

"Sure, I've known Bertram Bradley Oglethorpe Ogilvy since grade one. Why?"

"I was visiting Bryan Ogilvy tonight, and his father sort of mentioned you. It didn't sound as if he really knew you, though."

"He knows me, and I know him only too well."

"What does he do? He seems really rich."

"He doesn't *do* anything. He never has, and yes, he's very, very rich. He's C. Wilberforce Willson's great-nephew. Through his mother he inherited all the old boy's money when he was twelve, and he's been an absolute jerk ever since."

"He sure is rude and unpleasant," Casey told his dad as he stacked the folding bridge chairs. "By the way, Bryan Ogilvy's coming over tomorrow afternoon. He might want to talk to you."

"Oh, really?" His dad looked surprised. "That's interesting."

Neither Casey nor his father could have guessed just how interesting it was going to be.

CHAPTER SIX

"Mom and Dad, you remember Bryan Ogilvy?" Casey had answered Bryan's doorbell ring on Saturday afternoon and taken him right into the living room.

Casey's mother smiled at Bryan. "Hi, Bryan! Nice to see you. Casey's dad and I have known your father for a long time."

"How do you do?" Bryan shook hands stiffly.

"I was telling Casey last night that I started grade one with your father," Casey's dad said. "We haven't met your mother, though. She's from ...?"

"Montreal," Bryan offered. "Dad met her when he was at McGill University."

"I didn't realize your father had gone to university," Casey's father said, amazed. "Somehow I thought he'd stayed here all his life."

"Well," Bryan said, "he went to McGill but just long enough to meet my mother."

Casey's dad nodded.

"Bryan and I have things we need to do, so we're going upstairs now," Casey announced to his parents.

"When you're done, come down for something to eat," his mother suggested.

"Sounds good." Casey glanced at Bryan, who nodded and smiled thanks.

Bryan followed Casey up the stairs.

"Where did we leave off, Bryan?" Casey asked as they settled into chairs across from each other after Casey closed his bedroom door.

"Have I told you about the music yet?"

"No. What kind of music?"

"Hate music. White power rock and roll. It's got violent lyrics that call for murdering black people or starting a holy war. Anybody surfing the Net can find sites selling hate music or offering it free for downloading."

Casey whistled. "Really? Did you buy any?"

"I bought a few, and I've done some research on the music," Bryan admitted. "They sell huge numbers of white power CDs every year in North America. I bought some, like I say, but I didn't 'buy' into them, if you know what I mean."

"Yesterday you told me the online group asked you to steal for them and that they said they'd tell your parents and the police about the stealing and the drugs if you didn't do the next thing they wanted. So what did you do?"

"I distributed hate propaganda — some of the stuff you found in the Old Willson Place and ... and ..."

"And what?"

"I made that pipe bomb they used on the Finegoods' store. I got instructions off the Web."

"But you're only a kid!" Casey cried. "Nobody's going to get a thirteen-year-old to make a bomb!"

"They think I'm nineteen," Bryan said, "and I told them I knew how to make one."

"Have *they* ever seen you? Have you ever seen *them*?"

"No."

"Do you know who they are?"

Bryan hesitated, then said, "No. But they know *my* name. There's a mail drop where I pick up and leave stuff — a locker at the bus depot. They sent me a key to it. The thing is, Casey, I know telling you about all this isn't good enough. I know I should tell my parents. Only I just can't."

Casey knew there was only one way to go — talk to *his* dad — but it was up to Bryan to decide. "There's no way *I* can help you."

Bryan gazed out the window sadly. "Do you think I could talk to your father instead of the local Mounties?"

"Sure." Casey was glad he had already mentioned the possibility to his father. "My dad will know what to do." He opened his bedroom door and went to the head of the stairs. "Dad, can you come up here for a minute?"

Bryan and Casey's father talked for half an hour. At one point Casey's mother came into the room with a tray of sandwiches and cookies and a jug of hot cocoa.

Casey's dad took the tray. "I was just going to call you, Mary. You've got good instincts about things like this."

"Things like what?" she asked. "Is Casey involved in something?"

"No, it's Bryan," Chief Superintendent Templeton said. "Here's what's going on." Casey's mother listened to the point-by-point report of Bryan's involvement in the hate group.

"His parents have to be told *now*," she said, turning to Bryan. "Can you do that on your own, Bryan, or do you want one of us to come with you?"

"I don't know," Bryan said anxiously. "My dad can be very difficult."

"Your dad doesn't frighten me," Casey's mother said. "I'd be happy to come with you. Wait a minute. There's the phone." She went out and up to the master bedroom level. When she returned, she was smiling. "That was your father, Bryan, telling me you're to come home immediately for supper. I told him he'd have to wait until you're ready to come home, and that when you were ready I'd drive you and come in to talk to him."

"You said that? To my father?"

She smiled knowingly. "That's not all I said."

"Well, looks like problem number one is solved," Casey's father said. "Problem two is trickier. The local Mounties have to know what you've been up to, Bryan, or the hate group will keep trying to blackmail you."

A tear rolled down Bryan's cheek. "My parents will absolutely kill me."

"No, Bryan," Casey's mother told him, "they won't. They'll want to keep a tight lid on your adventures, that's for sure."

Casey pictured the wheels turning in his father's mind.

"Now about your distributing hate literature," the chief superintendent said, "and keeping the drugs they sent you and making a weapon, well, that falls within the mandate of the current Hate Cell investigation. Since I'm co-directing that investigation, it's up to me and Staff Sergeant Deblo what will be done about it. You've got to bring me everything you've ever received from this group or from the Web and anything you might still receive, and you've got to promise not to involve yourself further in any of this hate madness."

"I know it looks as if I was getting into it awfully deep," Bryan said," and I was, of course, but, honestly, I didn't really believe all their propaganda and I knew what I was doing was wrong."

Casey's dad smiled at Bryan. "Son, you proved that by your being here and trying to sort things out. You've done something really stupid, but I think you know that. Mrs. Templeton will drive you home now.

After you tell your parents, let her field their arguments." He glanced at his wife. "Mary, don't worry about supper. Casey and I will order in Chinese."

After they were gone, Casey told his father, "You and Mom handled that great!"

"Casey, your mother brought up four boys almost single-handedly. She's dealt with every sort of situation, I'd say, except maybe one like this. As for me, well, I've dealt with problems like this my entire career."

"Were you surprised, Dad, that Bryan was enlisted and trusted by this hate group?"

"No, I wasn't surprised. They thought he was nineteen, and they're on the lookout for intelligent young people with good communication skills. They need more than just thugs to beat up people. They need brains to help with their sophisticated networks."

"How did they get people to join up before the Web?"

"It wasn't nearly so easy," his dad said. "The hate groups used to distribute pamphlets on school grounds and in mailboxes, but they ran into intervention by teachers and parents. With the Web they've got a method to target young people directly, and unfortunately the Internet's a good way for them to look for future leaders."

"They're smart, aren't they?"

"Real smart," his father said. "See, they don't just target bright, affluent kids like Bryan. They also search for young people with traditional working-class goals and for the lonely, marginalized, and alienated — people who need to belong to something."

"That's what appealed to Bryan, right? He wanted to be accepted by someone."

His father sighed. "Emotionally vulnerable is the way people who analyze this hate business put it."

"I was wondering if there's any way Bryan could be part of your investigation, Dad ..."

"No, that's out of the question. Now let's get something to eat. All this talk has made me real hungry. Where's that delivery menu?"

CHAPTER SEVEN

The day after Casey had met Sarah Vance in Fraserville the snowstorms clobbering Richford for weeks finally headed south. With no shovelling to be done, he had some free time. Since Sarah wouldn't have any news for him for a week, Casey put that part of his investigation on hold. He stayed for basketball after school and went to the Ducks and Drakes with Hank a couple of times, beating his brother twice at Demon Explorer. To outdo Hank at anything concerning computers or video games was a miracle. Whenever there was a news item about hackers breaking into a top-secret computer, Casey felt uneasy, and he caught his parents giving Hank funny looks. Everyone would breathe a great sigh of relief when word came that the hackers had been caught, but then there was always the next time ...

Life was certainly more pleasant for Casey since the business with Mr. Deverell. Lots of people at school talked to him now, and being asked to be a member of the Coyote Club was great. But he knew some people were jealous of all the attention he was getting. Casey knew that it was almost worse to be at the top of the teeter-totter than at the bottom. It was so easy for whatever was holding you up there to move away and let you crash down. He had never wanted to be seen as anyone special; he only wanted to be seen.

Kevin and Terry had been with him when Steven Priddie had asked Casey sarcastically, "You planning to pose for any more publicity photos, Mr. Town Hero?" Greta Maitland, another student, then had made a nasty remark about how some new kids in town would do anything to impress people.

"What's with you two?" Kevin had demanded angrily. "You'd rather Mr. D. hadn't been found? That he'd died?"

"Well," Steve had replied, "if Old Deverell had minded his own business he wouldn't have gotten hurt."

Casey now figured he better get some of the other kids in on his investigation to share the spotlight if it shone again. But for sure not Steve Priddie. No. More like Kevin and Terry. They had been the first guys to show him any friendship, and he knew they and their families were just as upset about the hate situation as the Templetons were.

Bryan should be someone to involve in his investigation, too, but when he remembered the expression on his dad's face after he asked about letting Bryan assist in the inquiries, he decided that wasn't a good idea at all.

Casey was thinking about all of this while he and Bryan were walking home from school one day. In fact, he was on the verge of asking what had happened the night his mother had taken Bryan home. As if reading his mind, Bryan asked, "Want to hear what happened between your mother and my parents the other night?"

"Sure."

Bryan shook his head. "I couldn't believe it. When I told my parents about my involvement with the hate business, my dad started yelling and my mother began crying. Your mother, in a voice that was like ice and fire at the same time, told my dad to be quiet. Then she turned to my mother and told her how she and your father had been friends with my dad from when they were little kids. That even your grandparents and my grandparents had been friends.

"My dad glared at your mother, but she and my mom started to talk. My mother told yours not to blame the mess I got myself into all on my father, that a lot of it was her fault because her own mother died when she was only six and she'd never had anyone as a model for being a mother.

"I never heard my mother say anything like that ever. Your mother looked at her real sad and told my mother what a lot she'd missed and that she'd lost her father when she was thirteen and went ballistic with grief. She said it was your dad who'd helped her get through it."

"My mother said that?" Casey asked. "Boy, I never heard about that."

"Anyway, your mom told mine just to remember what she'd wished her mother could have done for her and to act like that toward me. Then your mother said they only had my side of this story and that there must have been some reason for me to have gotten involved the way I did. 'We always gave him everything he ever wanted,' my mother said sort of helplessly. 'Just like my father gave me everything.'

"Then your mother said something like, 'He needs love. And he needs to feel like he's a really an important part of your family.' Then she told my father what a great kid *he'd* been before he got all his money. My dad tried to interrupt, but your mother just went on. 'Up to now,' she said, 'it seems all you wanted Bryan for was so you could keep your money in the family. End of lecture.' My dad actually started spluttering, then said, 'How dare you talk to us like that!' Your mother just laughed and said she'd be on his tail if he didn't start paying attention to me. Then my mother asked yours if she'd like some coffee, and your mother said she'd like that fine."

Casey grinned. He sure had one heck of a mother.

84

X X X

A day or so later Casey persuaded Bryan to come to the Rec Hall. At first Bryan just stood inside the doorway chewing his fingernails, but Casey brought Marcie Finegood up to talk to him, and some of the others started including him in various activities.

As Casey, Kevin, and Terry walked to the Rec Hall that Friday, Casey said, "I've been wondering if you guys might like to help me with something to do with the Deverell case."

Kevin and Terry exchanged looks and nodded in unison, then Kevin asked, "Are you involved in the investigation?"

"Not officially, but I'm working on a couple of ideas. Want to hear?"

"Sure," Terry said.

Casey told them about finding the drapery remnant and his contact with Sarah Vance. He didn't tell them anything he had picked up listening to his dad and the RCMP talking, or what he knew about Hank's research. Casey kept strictly to his own discoveries.

"If Sarah can get the names and addresses of who bought the fabric," he told them, "maybe the three of us can check them out. The weather's too bad to bicycle around the countryside, but maybe we can come up with a way to see the necessary places."

"My brother, Jeff, just got his driver's licence," Kevin said. "He'll drive anyone anywhere, and he was Mr. Deverell's star student and good friend a few years ago. I know he'd want to help find who clobbered him."

"Terrific!" Casey said. "Tell him my dad's co-directing the team of investigators. I might hear something from Sarah by tomorrow night. I'll let you know. And, guys — this is strictly between us and Jeff, okay?"

"Absolutely," Terry said. "I'm glad we get to help. But that's just one thing. You said you had a couple of ideas."

"Either of you got any connections to Sanford's Hardware?" Casey asked. Then he told them about the brass screws.

"I've got connections," Terry admitted. "All the wrong kind. My aunt used to be married to one of the Sanfords, and since they broke up, the families haven't talked. Now my dad goes way out of town for all his hardware."

"I don't know anybody there at all," Kevin said.

Casey frowned. "Too bad. Keep thinking."

"Okay," Kevin said as he held open the door of the Rec Hall for the others to enter.

Everyone at the Rec Hall was talking about the school's Halloween costume party coming up in a week. Bryan was there, just inside the door again, speaking to Marcie Finegood. Casey hoped they weren't getting too friendly, because he thought of Marcie as *his* very good friend and maybe something more. The party wasn't a "boy asks girl" or "girl asks boy" thing. It was just a great big party the school held every year for kids too old to go trick-or-treating. Every year more and more kids from Casey's high school came. It was *the* place to be. Casey was surprised at the enthusiasm. He had never been at a school where even the parents — who came to dish out food, play heavy metal, rock and rap, give out prizes, and even stand watch over a dozen rented video game machines — wore costumes and masks so that nobody was sure who was who.

When Bryan and Marcie noticed Casey and his new friends, they came over. Casey caught Bryan looking at him warily, as if he thought Casey might spill the beans about what had happened. *He should know I'd never do that,* Casey thought.

"So do you guys wear costumes at the Halloween party?" Casey asked.

"You have to or you don't get into the party," Kevin said.

Casey had a sudden vision of what he would go as. It was so brilliant he almost told Terry and Kevin right there. But he decided he would keep it a secret. He was going to go as Mr. Clarence Wilberforce Willson!

Marcie had taken Bryan to talk to two girls at a table across the Rec Hall. She glanced up and waved at Casey.

"See you guys later," Casey said to Kevin and Terry. "There's something I want to ask Marcie about."

"Sure thing," Terry said.

"You going to be back soon?" Kevin asked. "Remember, we've reserved the pool table for eight o'clock. That's just ten minutes from now."

"I'll be back," Casey said, threading his way through the Friday night crush toward Marcie. "So, Marcie," he said when he reached her and led her to a bench away from the others, "how are things? No more posters of swastikas, I hope."

"No more of those," Marcie said, "but my dad's been getting awful phone calls telling him to leave town so people who belong here can breathe the pure air of freedom. Freedom from *us*, I guess." She was mad. "They're not going to scare me, Casey, no way. My family's been in this area almost a hundred years. We've always been good citizens, paid our taxes, everything, and now some people are telling us to leave. They think they can scare us? Let 'em try!"

"Did your dad tell the RCMP about the phone calls?"

"No. He's mad as heck about it, but the callers said they'd torch our store again if we reported the calls. Dad says it's not worth putting our family at risk, that nothing can be done." She was silent for a moment. "Look, I'm telling you, Casey, because I know your father's trying to stop these terrible things. You tell him what's happening. I'm sure he can do something."

"I'm sure he can, too," Casey assured her. "I'll tell him."

Marcie pointed across the room. "Your friends are trying to get your attention."

"Yeah, we have something set up." Casey got to his feet. "By the way, are you going to the Halloween party?"

"Everyone goes to the Halloween party," Marcie said matter-of-factly.

"Well, uh, I ... I guess I'll see you there for sure," Casey said nervously, then made his way hurriedly to the pool table at the other end of the hall.

XXX

The problem of tracking down the brass screws was on Casey's mind as he walked home from the Rec Hall later that night. He was feeling pretty good about himself, feeling like one of the gang, feeling as if he could solve anything. Well, almost everything, except maybe the business of the phone calls to Marcie's dad. If Terry, Kevin, and he could come up with information that either solved the case of Mr. Deverell or at least pushed it forward, that would be terrific. It would show the Mounties and his father that they were wrong to turn down his help.

Then something else occurred to him. What if he could make a copy of the police artist's sketch of "Elsie Tavich." He could take it to Sanford's Hardware and see if someone remembered her buying the screws. Of course, she might not have been involved except in connection with the computer. But what if the Hate Cell used her so that none of their members would be seen around Richford?

Casey's father was sitting at the kitchen table surrounded by heaps of papers as Casey came in the back door. "Hi, Dad!"

"Hello, Casey. You've had two phone calls, both from the same woman, I think. Your mother took one and I took the other."

Casey tried to sound uninterested. "Really? I wonder if it was Mrs. Phipps at the library."

"At ten-fifteen? I don't think so."

Since it didn't sound as if his father was going to pursue the subject, Casey decided to change it. "Doing some homework on the Deverell case, Dad?"

"I'm looking over what we have so far. What really puzzles me is the fact that we can't find a trace of anyone around here who might be involved. Whoever they are, they must have taken off — far off."

"I heard something new from Marcie Finegood, something her dad's afraid to tell your team because he's been threatened with another fire if he does. But Marcie said I should tell you because she thinks you can and will do something about it."

"Tell me."

Casey filled him in on the phone calls point by point.

"This is so important, Casey. We'll get phone taps on the Finegoods' phones right away."

"But Marcie's father will have a fit if he finds out she's told us."

"Leave Mr. Finegood to me, Casey. This might be the only way we can track these people down."

Casey spotted a stack of posters with the face of a woman blown up on them. He knew who it was, but he acted as if he didn't. "Who's that?"

"That's Elsie Tavich. She's tied into this business, but she's proving very difficult to trace. She hasn't been using any credit cards as far as we can tell. It's as if she vanished."

"Any way I can help?" Casey asked innocently, scooping up a couple of the posters. "I could ask around at school and maybe check out the library. I'm sure Mrs. Phipps would put one up on the bulletin board."

To Casey's surprise, his father said, "Why not? It's worth trying. Take as many copies as you like. It always pays to be thorough. And speaking of being thorough, I'm sure you noticed the wind's blown a lot of snow back onto the sidewalk and driveway. I guess you'll be busy fixing that tomorrow morning, right?"

"Right," Casey groaned. He opened the fridge and took out a foil-wrapped plate of fried chicken legs. "Want some, Dad?" He put three of the eight on a plate for himself and sat down.

"That sounds like a good idea," his dad admitted.

Casey put three chicken legs on a second plate and took out the breadboard, a knife, a loaf of caraway rye, butter, a carton of milk, and two glasses. The food disappeared quickly.

"I'll have just one more leg, Casey."

"And I'll have the last one," Casey said, taking them out of the fridge.

"Oh-oh!" his dad said. "Weren't they supposed to be for tomorrow's lunch?"

"Yeah, I think so."

They finished off the chicken in happy silence.

"Tell you what," his dad said finally, looking full, satisfied, and younger than Casey could remember in a long time. "I'll invite your mother out for lunch tomorrow to the Snick Snack. Want to come?"

Casey grinned. "Sure, Dad." He was thinking how he would do the sidewalks, take in lunch at the Snick Snack, and then start his research at Sanford's Hardware.

CHAPTER EIGHT

"So," Casey's dad asked, "what will we have for lunch?"

Casey and his parents were early enough at the Snick Snack to get the best booth, the one with a big window overlooking Main Street, which hadn't changed much in seventy years. It featured single-storey stores and restaurants, most with false fronts, as well as sturdy two-storey brick or poured concrete buildings from the turn of the century through the booming 1920s. Buildings with their pioneer owners' names were proudly announced in insets or in sculpted concrete. Richford's Main Street was typical of the Prairies, especially since the small town's new mall was safely out of sight on a side street.

Their table's bright yellow Formica top matched the lunch counter on the far side of the restaurant, with its tall stools covered in yellow plastic. The linoleum floor had once been yellow, too. It still was in the corners. The last of the morning coffee drinkers, a quartet of farmers in peaked caps, were draining their cups.

"Let's hear what their Saturday special is," Casey's mother suggested. "If it's ribs, that's for me."

"Me, too," Casey said. He had held back at break-fast, knowing lunch would be really something. Word in town was that, while Ducks and Drakes might be the best restaurant in Richford during the week, on Saturday afternoon the *only* place to eat was the Snick Snack.

"Well, I don't feel like ribs." Casey's father sig-nalled the waitress. "Hi, Tammy, what's for lunch?"

A pretty blond waitress in a pink-and-white-striped uniform with matching cap brought over a small blackboard with SPECIALS printed in multico-loured chalk across the top. "Well, ribs, is one special."

"Casey and I want ribs for sure," Mrs. Templeton said.

"With coleslaw or Caesar?" Tammy asked.

"Coleslaw for me," they both said together.

Casey's dad frowned as he read the menu. "Everything sounds so good."

Tammy waited patiently. She had had the Tem-pletons for lunch many times before and knew there was no point in trying to hurry the chief su-perintendent.

"Ah ..." he began.

Casey and his mother glanced at each other and raised their eyebrows with a "Here we go again" smile.

"Aha!" Casey's dad said.

Tammy shifted the blackboard to her other hip.

"Yes!" he said.

Everyone held their collective breaths.

"It's got to be the goulash. You know, the Croatians in Bosnia used to make absolutely fabulous goulash."

"Hope ours measures up," Tammy said as she went off to place their orders. "I'll hear about it for sure if it doesn't."

Casey sat back as Tammy put hot rolls and butter on the table. He had just begun buttering a roll when his mother asked, "Tell us, Casey, who's this woman who's been phoning you?"

There was no way to get out of this one, so Casey said, "Oh, it's Sarah Vance. You met her at her dad's drape shop in Fraserville, Mom. She's the one you asked all the questions about dying drapes."

"Yes, I remember her. But why is she phoning you?"

"It all has to do with a paper she's writing for a sociology class at university. See, she recognized me as the person who'd helped save Mr. Deverell and unearthed the Hate Cell business. She's done a lot of research on racism in Canada, the United States, and Europe and was surprised that a hate group was operating right here."

"And what does she think you can tell her that

she can't read in the newspaper?" Casey's father asked, looking sternly at his son.

"Beats me." Casey shrugged, praying Tammy would bring their food soon. He thought he had better say something more, so he added, "Look, guys, Sarah's really nice and pretty and smart. A part of why I want to get to know her better is so I can somehow have Hank meet her. Honestly, I think they'd really hit it off. And then maybe Hank would come out of himself and ... and, well, you know ..."

His mother nodded as Tammy put a large plate of ribs with baked potato and coleslaw in front of her. "I know what you mean, Casey. I hope you can make it work."

Casey's father nodded his agreement, too.

"She reminds me so much of Cindy," Casey told them. "I have this feeling Hank will think so, too."

Eating ribs wasn't something you could do and talk much at the same time. Casey finished first and gazed out the big window, watching what counted as crowds strolling down Main Street. A long line was forming both inside the restaurant and out. Two couples at the front of the line kept glancing anxiously at the Templetons' table. Casey hoped Tammy would stop by with their bill so his dad would get the hint and hurry it up a bit.

Finally, they were done, the bill was paid, and Casey was free to do his research at Sanford's Hardware. "See you at supper," he said as his parents started walking arm in arm toward their house.

"At six," his dad said. "And don't be late."

Casey's dad always said you could tell a lot about a small town by its hardware store. He said a well-stocked shop would bring in townsfolk and farmers, mechanics and hobbyists, gardeners and fence builders, gadget lovers and cooks, and all the others, both men and women, who just liked to look at all the different stuff.

The building housing Sanford's Hardware was a hundred years old. It was built of brick and was cool inside even on the hottest days. It smelled pleasantly of dark plank floors, saws and hammers, hedge clippers and spades, drills and wrenches, all rubbed with a film of oil to keep them from rusting. Long ropes of different thicknesses coiled down from the embossed tin ceiling, and huge black scoop-shaped vats held heaps of nuts and bolts. Casey loved it. You could go in the front door, take a shortcut through to the side door, and see a million interesting things en route. It seemed to have everything. Never mind that the bigger towns had big box stores. The Sanfords had owned their shop for eighty-four years, and their customer service was legendary.

Some people said Sanford's would hire a taxi within a radius of a hundred and sixty kilometres to pick up something if it were needed in Richford the next day, but Casey's dad told him that wasn't true. The Sanfords were such a big family that they had relatives in every town and village for kilometres around and would start a grapevine going among all their kin to look for a desired item. When it was located, and it almost always was, the finders would, if they couldn't mail it or ship it by bus for arrival the next day, be invited to bring it and their family to Richford for a meal.

Customer satisfaction was so high that Sanford's had expanded into four other stores on Main Street. Even so, it was always full, especially on a fine Saturday in any season.

Casey pushed his way through the crowd to Mr. Sanford's office and waited his turn to speak to the "boss." Mr. Sanford didn't recognize the picture of Elsie Tavich, but he checked on when the other six screws had been sold. He called his salespeople up one by one in case anybody recognized the face in the picture.

No one did, but Casey did discover that one employee might have served Elsie Tavich but was no longer with the store. Millie Anne Brighton, who now lived in White Rock, British Columbia, had worked at Sanford's during the time in question.

Casey returned to Mr. Sanford's office to thank him personally, but two men he didn't recognize were talking to the boss. Casey was near enough to hear and curious enough not to move away.

"Yeah," one of the men said," I heard it not ten minutes ago. Ole Hanson's had a stroke."

"My God!" Mr. Sanford said. "Not Ole. He's been mayor of Richford how long now?"

"Sixteen years," the second man said. "Of course, he's still mayor, stroke or no stroke, but if he's incapacitated, who is there to take his place?"

"Well, we all know who *wants* to be mayor," Mr. Sanford said. "He ran against Ole years ago."

"Yeah, and got about a dozen votes," the first man said. "B.B.O. Ogilvy bought every one of them, too."

"That's what he'll try to do this time, too," the second man said. "We've got to get another candidate who can beat him the way Ole did."

"Ole's a straight-up guy," Mr. Sanford said. "Honest as the day is long." -

"Right," the first man agreed. "Sure hope he comes out of this okay."

Casey didn't want to be caught eavesdropping, so he went right up to the office door and waved a hand at Mr. Sanford.

"You want something, Casey?" Mr. Sanford asked.

"Just to say thanks for taking the time to help."

"No problem. It's very important that we find out what's going on around here. It's a black eye for the whole town."

Casey left the shop and stood outside on the sidewalk, his mind racing. He had the answer to how his dad could stay and be happy in Richford: Chief Superintendent Templeton could be the mayor! His father would be a natural with all his experience and people skills. And Casey was certain almost everyone in town would vote for his dad. It sure didn't sound as if many would vote for Mr. Ogilvy. Casey wondered how a person could "buy" votes in a town like Richford.

Now all he had to do was plant the seed. He would

get his mother onside. She would know the right way to suggest running for mayor to his father. Brilliant!

X X X

Casey spent the time after the visit to Sanford's Hardware assembling his costume for the Halloween party. He had taken a photograph of the portrait of old C.W. Willson that hung in the school library, a picture of the old boy with a black frock coat and black trousers, a tall hat, a high white wing collar with a silk cravat held in place by a large diamond stick pin, a vest with a heavy watch chain across it, grey hair, a thick moustache, and a large black mole on his chin.

For a couple of dollars at a second-hand store in Richford, Casey bought a black suit that had a vest and cut the back to look like tails, then trimmed the sleeves so that they were the right length. He also picked up a lady's black silk scarf for his cravat and a single phony diamond earring for his tie pin. There were no wing-collar shirts at the second-hand store, of course, but there was one with a stiffly starched collar. Casey studied it for a long time until he figured how he could cut and fold it so it would look just right. He made a silk hat out of black construction paper, bought a huge moustache and a grey wig from Grant's Variety Store, and experimented with sticking a piece of licorice to his chin. Now all he had to do was put the business cards inscribed with Clarence Wilberforce Willson, publisher, *Richford*

Weekly Mirror, in his pocket and hide everything in the back of his closet. Hank, whom he had sworn to secrecy, had made the cards for him.

X X X

As the Templetons were finishing up a light supper of soup and sandwiches, the telephone rang.

"It's a female for you, Casey," Hank called from the hall. "Nice voice."

It had to be Sarah, Casey thought as he got up to take the call. Why was she calling him now? He had left her a voice mail message after lunch at the Snick Snack, saying that he would call her in the evening. Casey left the kitchen, went into the hall, and took the portable phone from Hank. "Casey Templeton here."

"Hi, it's Sarah. I'm going to a movie, so I thought I'd call now. I've got a good news, bad news message."

"What?"

"First the good news. Only two customers bought that fabric from us. We had a huge order for drapes in that fabric from the Bible Institute a year ago. That's one. The second order, and here's the bad news, was paid for in cash. There's no record of any name. All we have is a telephone number to call when an order's ready. We're going to have to talk about what we do if you find out who it is."

"Yeah," Casey muttered.

"Somebody listening?" Sarah asked.

"Yeah."

"Call me right at noon tomorrow," Sarah said. "I'll be leaving at 12:15." She hung up.

"Nice voice," Hank said again, "but she sounds a little old for you. Anyone I'd like to know?"

"Maybe," Casey told him.

"Let's see. You used exactly three words with the lady if I don't count your name. Here, what, and yeah. You're some conversationalist, bro'."

Casey didn't say anything. He was too busy trying to figure out how he could call Sarah at noon tomorrow with everyone hanging around the house for Sunday brunch. "Mom," he asked as he cleared the table, "why don't you take it easy after church tomorrow instead of making brunch? I'll leave for home right after the sermon, cook brunch for a change, and set it all up in the dining room."

Hank and his father stared at Casey in surprise, but his mom just smiled, gave him a hug, and said, "I'd really like that, Casey."

"No problem." Casey hugged her back.

CHAPTER NINE

Anybody could cook an omelette, Casey was thinking early the next morning as he took down his mother's well-worn *Joy of Cooking* and checked the index. He figured he would find out how to cook omelettes and get all the ingredients ready before church. After church he would have plenty of time to cook, phone Sarah at noon, and serve up the brunch of the decade.

As he read the section on omelettes, Casey realized there was a little more to it than he had imagined. He had been right, though, about leaving the ingredients out. Eggs were supposed to be at room temperature. But how many eggs and what kind of omelette? French didn't look too hard, but you had to make little ones and serve them right away. Fluffy? No way, with all that business of dividing the eggs and whipping the yolks and whites separately. He settled on something called firm omelettes — you could make big ones that way with up to ten eggs.

Casey cut a big piece of ham into small squares, diced some green onions, and cleaned and cut up a handful of mushrooms. That ought to do for the filling, he thought, then decided to make a salad. Fruit salad would be good with the omelette and with the bran muffins he had found in the freezer.

By the time the family left for church, Casey had the table set, the coffee ground, the salad made, and the muffins defrosting. All he had to do was make the omelette — no problem.

✗ ✗ ✗

Would the sermon never end? It was already twenty past eleven. Finally, Casey could leave. He had brought his coat with him so he could make a quick exit. It took only five minutes to run home.

Casey had seen the chefs on television break eggs one-handed into a bowl. With a big glass bowl at the ready, he took an egg in his right hand and gave it a sharp crack on the rim of the bowl. White, yolk, and shell slid slowly down the outside of the bowl to the table, then gradually from the table onto Casey's shoe. It took time to wipe up the mess.

He held the second egg with both hands, made a clean break, gripped the split shell, and let the white and yolk pour into the bowl. Nothing to it once he got the hang of it. The shell of the third egg splintered as Casey cracked it, and pieces fell into the bowl. By the time he had picked all the bits out of the liquid, Casey was getting nervous. There were just a dozen eggs, one had fallen, and he needed ten. He had to be very careful. Casey took down a saucer from a cupboard and cracked each egg into it before he slid it into the big bowl. He beat the eggs until blended and then beat in the water, salt, and paprika he had assembled earlier.

Now he had to melt butter into a skillet. The recipe called for four eggs and one and a half tablespoons of butter. He had used ten eggs, so he needed two times one and a half tablespoons. That was three tablespoons plus half of one and a half, which was three-quarters. So he had to melt three and three-quarter tablespoons of butter in the skillet. He already had a skillet on the stove, so he turned the heat on low under it and put the butter in.

Next he got the fruit salad out of the fridge, put the plates in the oven to warm, placed the bran muffins on top of the plates, poured the orange juice, and was setting up the coffee as the front door opened.

"How are you doing, Casey?" his mom asked from the living room.

"Fine!" Casey shouted. "But stay out of here till I call. About five minutes, okay?"

Casey went back to the stove, turned the gas up under the skillet, watched until the butter was bubbling, and poured the egg mixture into the pan.

There it was. In the pan. But what he was supposed to do next? He rushed to where he had left the *Joy of Cooking* open on the counter and started to read.

"Cook over low heat," the book said. Casey reduced the gas to simmer. "Lift the edge with a pancake turner and tilt the skillet to permit the uncooked custard to run to the bottom, or stick it with a fork in the soft spots to permit the heat to penetrate the bottom crust. When it is all of even consistency, fold the omelette over and serve it."

Frantically, Casey tilted the pan and tried to raise a corner of the paper-thin layer of omelette. The whole thing rushed toward him. He righted the pan and poked the mixture with a fork. Whatever had finally thickened on the bottom ripped. Maybe he had turned the heat down too much. He put the heat on high, and in seconds smelled something burning. At medium high it still appeared to be burning. Finally, at low again, the omelette seemed to be cooking right. But what about the filling? And how to turn the darn thing over?

Casey shook the filling mixture over the mountains and valleys of omelette, slid the pancake turner under one side, and began easing it over. The part he was flipping split from the rest, but he had gotten a good-sized piece turned. To his horror he saw that the whole bottom side of what he had folded over was black. Casey grabbed a paring knife out of the dish rack, carefully cut off the burned part, turned it over, sliced off the other burned surface, divided what he had flipped into two portions, placed them on hot plates, and called, "Ready!" As his family sat down in the dining room, Casey brought in two plates. "Mom and Dad, please start. I'll have yours ready in a couple of minutes, Hank."

"Smells good," Casey's dad said, smacking his lips.

"Sure does," his mom agreed, taking a taste and reaching for the ketchup.

"Why don't you start on your salad, Hank?" Casey suggested.

Back in the kitchen, Casey looked at the mess in the pan. He pulled out what he could of the burned bits, picked up the rest, formed it into a pie section, put it on a plate, took it into the dining room, covered it with ketchup, and set it before Hank. His brother had a computer magazine in front of him and didn't seem to notice anything wrong.

"Not bad, Casey," Hank said. "A little dry here and there, but not bad."

"Not having any, Casey?" his mother asked.

Casey sighed. "No. I've had enough of omelettes for a long time." *Time!* He glanced at the clock. Twelve-fifteen! He had forgotten to call Sarah. Now it was too late. She would think he didn't care enough to phone. Casey helped himself to a bowl of fruit salad and took a bran muffin. All that work for nothing!

X X X

"Well?" Kevin asked the next day as he, Terry, and Casey were getting into their basketball workout clothes. "Did you hear from what's-her-name?"

"I heard part of what she found out," Casey said. "She does have the number and some other stuff to tell me, but …"

"But what?" Terry pressed.

Casey told them about the brunch fiasco. "I was just too smart for my own good, and now I'm afraid Sarah's mad and maybe won't give me the number. If she doesn't, that's it."

"Can't you leave her a voice mail message and explain?" Kevin asked. "She probably checks her messages."

"I did phone last night and left a message, but she didn't call back. I'll let you know if I do hear from her. Oh, and I should tell you that you don't have to worry about Sanford's."

"Why not?" Terry asked.

"Well, by a fluke I got this." He took a poster out of his backpack. "This is a woman who's involved with the whole Hate Cell business. My dad said I could show her picture around at school and take another one for Mrs. Phipps to put up in the library. Well, I had it with me Saturday afternoon and I took it into Sanford's in case someone there remembered selling those long brass screws to her."

"And?" Terry asked.

Casey told them about his conversation with Mr. Sanford and that no one recalled selling the screws. "But someone did mention that Millie Anne Brighton was working there at the time but had moved to White Rock, British Columbia."

"That's the aunt I told you about," Kevin said.

"I wondered if it was," Casey said. "Do you know her phone number?"

"I can get it easy," Kevin said. "I'll call you later."

"Have you thought of any other things we could investigate?" Terry asked as they walked to the gym.

"Not really," Casey said, "except how Mr. D. got involved. Ask your folks, casually like, what they know about him. He sure didn't seem the kind of guy to go messing about in that kind of operation."

"Will you three hurry up, please?" Mr. Tate, the basketball coach, shouted. "We've only got the gym for an hour today, and there's just a week till the county tournament!"

"I'll let you know if I do hear from Sarah," Casey said as the three sprinted toward the court.

X X X

Hank turned around in his chair. "There's a letter for you, Casey. You never get letters except from Grandma. It doesn't have a return address, but it was postmarked in Edmonton. Who's it from?"

"How do I know till I open it? Where is it?"

"Mom put it on the kitchen table, I think."

"So Mom knows about it?" Casey asked.

"Sure, and Dad saw it, too. We're all dying to know who it's from. I'm betting on that voice on the phone. If it's her, you better watch it. Like I said, she sounds too old for you."

"Will you please go back up to your computer, Hank? It's my business, not yours, so stuff it."

"Is that you, Casey?" his mom called from the kitchen. "There's a letter for you from Edmonton."

Casey ambled into the kitchen, put his backpack on the table, and sat down. "May I have some of those?" He pointed at a plate heaped with small cream-covered crescents. "Whatever they are."

"Help yourself. They're for the school bake sale, but I can spare a couple. Aren't you going to open your letter?"

"No," Casey said. His hand itched to reach out and tear the letter open. It had to be from Sarah.

"Hank thinks it's from the girl who called you on Friday and Saturday. He seems very interested in Sarah."

Casey smiled with satisfaction. "Good. If the letter's from Sarah, it'll be about her sociology project." He picked up the letter and his backpack and climbed the stairs to his room. Sprawling on his bed, he opened the envelope and took out a single page. The message *was* from Sarah:

I gather you couldn't call me. Here's the phone number Vance's called when the drapes were ready, and here are the dimensions of the drapes Vance's made for that order. You'd better check that they're an exact fit for the window in question before you take matters any further. Good luck, and keep me posted.

Sarah's university residence address, the phone number, and the dimensions of the drapes were included on the single page.

"Wow!" Casey said to himself. He had his second clue — something none of the other investigators had. All he had to do was check the size of the window at the Old Willson Place, and if it matched the measurements Sarah had sent him, he would get Kevin's brother to take them out to the address of the person who had ordered the drapes once they had it. He was pretty sure it was a regional phone number. On Friday, instead of going to the Rec Hall, he, Terry, and Kevin could track down who the number belonged to in the area telephone books at the C.W. Willson Public Library. On Saturday Jeff could drive them to the address of the place whose phone number Sarah had sent.

Casey gazed out his window. He had almost lied to his mother. Well, if he solved things it would be a wonderful surprise for everyone, so maybe that covered his secrecy about the letter from Sarah. He could give the phone number to his father. In fact, he *should* give it his dad. His father and the Mounties could find out whose number it was in a matter of minutes. Hank could probably come up with it, too. But if the name was one they had already come across in the case, Hank would pass it on to Casey's father. His brother would have to, since he was getting paid to help out. But then Casey would be out of the loop. No, he, Terry, and Kevin would find the number and follow through. But he was going to need some help when he got the number of Millie Anne Brighton in White Rock. He would have to ask

Hank for assistance. Casey couldn't make the call because there was no way he could sound like a man, particularly since his voice kept squeaking. But first there was the phone number from Sarah to work on. The talk with Kevin's Aunt Millie would come later.

CHAPTER TEN

It wasn't easy, and it was boring. The three boys worked hard for two hours, sitting at a long table in the C.W. Willson Public Library and poring over area telephone books. Finally, Terry kneaded his forehead. "My eyes are sore, I'm getting a headache, and I'm sick of staring at numbers."

Casey looked at his friends. For them to give up even five minutes of their Friday night fun was a real sacrifice. It showed they really did care, just as much as he did, that the Hate Cell thugs got caught. "Let's give it half an hour more. If we don't find it by then, we'll quit."

Kevin yawned and stretched his arms. "And head to the Rec Hall for something to eat and drink, right?"

"Right," Terry agreed, and Casey nodded.

They had figured out a few things. The number didn't belong to Fraserville or its suburbs — each area had its own first three digits, and each town had its own first three digits, but things were different in the farm areas, and that was where this number must be. Before they had started, Casey had called the number from the library payphone and gotten voice mail that gave the phone number and "Leave your message after the beep" in a man's flat voice.

At the end of half an hour Terry and Kevin put on their jackets.

"I'll be right along," Casey told them. "I'm going to ask Mrs. Phipps if she has any ideas."

When he told the librarian what he was looking for, she said, "Well, it could be an unlisted number — that's the most likely thing. Or you boys might have missed it. How important is it that you find this number?"

"Very, very important, Mrs. Phipps."

"Well, I can't let you into the library computer, but if you tell me why you need the number, I'll scan down the list of people with library cards. There are about two-hundred and fifty names."

"It has to do with who almost killed Mr. Deverell," Casey said.

"Oh, I see. That was such a terrible thing. And those other incidents! The whole town's boiling. Stay around for a few minutes after closing time and I'll have a look."

Casey went back to the phone books. He found a number that was exactly the same except for the last digit and called it on the payphone. There was no answer.

"No luck, Casey," Mrs. Phipps said after the library closed.

"Thanks so much for trying," he told her. "I'll keep you posted."

It was twenty-five after nine by the time Casey left the library. He didn't feel like going to the Rec Hall. Instead he wanted to go home. Casey had thought it would be a breeze to find the number, but it hadn't been. So now what?

As soon as Casey got home, he went up to his room. When he passed Hank's bedroom, he heard his brother yelling at the computer. He was sure Hank could find who belonged to the phone number. His brother could unearth just about anything. But again Casey hesitated. Letting Hank in on what he was up to might freeze him out of the investigation, especially since his brother was doing research for the police. He would have to take a chance, though. Casey made himself a cheese sandwich, took out a can of cola, went back upstairs, flopped into a chair near Hank, and offered his brother half of the sandwich.

Hank took the sandwich and wolfed it down. "You're back early. I'm just on my way out."

"Stay, Hank. I need some help."

"What kind?"

"Computer kind. If all I have is a rural Alberta

phone number, how can I find whose it is and where they live?"

Hank shot Casey a knowing look. "Is this something to do with that letter? She writes you from Edmonton, but she lives around here, right?"

"You're so smart. Can you do it?"

"Not legally."

Casey wrote down the number. "When has that ever stopped you before?"

"What's in it for me?"

Casey thought for a moment. "I'll clear the supper table and do the dishes by myself every day for a month. And very soon I'll tell you all about who *she* is and how come *she* and I are working together."

"You're on!"

"Only one thing," Casey added, "you might find yourself in a sort of conflict-of-interest situation."

"I'll worry about that when it happens. Now go away. I'll call when I've got it, and I'd like another cheese sandwich, please, but this time with tomatoes, lettuce, and mayo."

Casey went downstairs, made another sandwich, brought it up to Hank, then returned to the living room, where his parents were watching television. His parents waved at him but didn't say anything. They were too wrapped up in the movie they were watching. In no time at all, though, Hank was shouting for him, and he rushed back upstairs.

As it turned out, the number belonged to an Alfred W. Sorum. Hank wrote out the site and rural route numbers for Casey on a slip of paper and gave it to him.

"Thanks a lot, Hank!"

"It was easy as pie," Hank said. "And real soon I get told everything about that girl, right?"

Casey nodded.

Hank put on his jacket and headed off for other challenges at the Ducks and Drakes. Casey heard him rev up his motorcycle and roar away.

X X X

On Tuesday of the next week Casey finally got a chance to tell Hank part of what was going on and to persuade him to make the phone call to Millie Anne Brighton in White Rock. This time he had to agree to make Hank's bed until Christmas and pay for the long-distance call when Hank got his cell phone bill. He gave Hank the number, and his brother punched it out on the phone.

"Why don't you go do something, Casey?" Hank said. "I'll let you know when I'm done."

Casey left his brother's bedroom, went to his own room, and flopped onto the bed. He thought about how costly this investigation was getting, how he was paying dearly in services for Hank, to say nothing of the time and money he was spending on various leads. A few minutes later Hank called him back into his bedroom.

"Well?" Casey asked, sitting on a chair.

"The woman thought I was absolutely nuts.

When I finally convinced her that it was her duty as a good citizen to try to help, she said, 'How am I supposed to remember one sale of six brass screws someone bought all that time ago?' So I asked her, 'Have you got a computer? I could send you her picture by email.' That seemed to make her think this wasn't some kind of stupid joke. So she said, 'Yeah, I have a computer,' and she gave me her email address. So I'm going to send her the sketch of Elsie Tavich and we'll see what happens."

Hank scanned the sketch and emailed it to Millie. About half an hour later they got an answer. Millie Anne Brighton didn't remember seeing the woman in the sketch, and try as she might, she couldn't recall selling anybody six long brass screws. Dead end, or so it seemed.

XXX

"Want to come up to Edmonton tomorrow, Casey?" his dad asked when Casey stopped by his parents' bedroom to say good-night the next Friday. "I thought we'd call Jake and Billy, try for some Oilers hockey tickets, and look for a TV for your bedroom. I agree it's a better use of money than some fancy window covers. We'll be leaving about nine in the morning tomorrow and we'll be back pretty late if we get the tickets to the game. If we don't, we'll probably be back by six."

Casey gave his mother a thumbs-up. "I'd love a TV, Dad. But I'll trust you to choose one for me. I've got a couple of things I want to do here tomorrow. But say hello to the guys for me."

His parents glanced at each other in surprise. This wasn't like Casey. He had never turned down a chance to go to an Oilers game before.

"Well, all right," his mother said. "Hank will be in charge." She clicked off the television in the bedroom. "And there's plenty to eat. We should say goodbye now in case you're not up by the time we leave."

"He'll be up," his dad declared.

"I will," Casey promised.

But he almost wasn't. He stayed up late, going over area maps he had gotten from his dad's study. By two o'clock Casey knew exactly where Alfred Sorum's place was and how to get there. He would phone Kevin and Jeff in the morning and set it all up. Casey wasn't sure what he would do when they found the place. Maybe there would be no one there. And if people were there, how could he ever find out if they were part of the gang that had attacked Mr. Deverell?

Even though he had a few qualms about the whole business, he still figured things were going well, so he hunched the duvet over his shoulders, yawned, and fell fast asleep.

X X X

As expected, Hank wasn't up when Casey's parents left for Edmonton the next morning. Casey wondered for the umpteenth time why Hank always got to sleep in while he had to be up to wave goodbye to the old folks. Of course, Casey knew the answer to that. Long ago he had figured out why his dad paid so much attention to him. For the growing up of his other three sons, Chief Inspector Templeton had been very busy or away. For Casey he was now on the spot. Every day. Always. Casey had to be perfect or else. He sighed, knowing how far from perfect he was or ever would be. Still, today he was glad he had to get up, because that meant he had the house to himself to call Kevin.

"Jeff can't get the car until around three this afternoon," Kevin told him on the phone. "Like you said to, he told our folks your dad approved of where we're going. But Jeff wants to know how long you figure to be gone and who's going to pay for the gas. He's spent ages figuring out routes and distances."

Casey did some quick calculations. It was a good forty kilometres to the Sorum place. That would take over half an hour. Add the return trip with a stop-over to check out the place — a minimum hour and a half. He told that to Kevin and that he would pay for the gas.

"Just a minute," Kevin said. "I'll check with Jeff."

Casey waited. This meant he would have to go to the Old Willson Place on his own to measure the window, but there was little danger that his parents would return to Richford before he did even if they didn't get the hockey tickets and arrived home by six. He should be back from the Sorum place well before that.

Kevin came back on the phone. "Jeff says okay. Be here at a quarter to three."

"I'll be there. Say thanks to Jeff."

As Casey put on extra socks under his boots and pulled on a second sweater, he figured he would go to the Old Willson Place the same way he had that first night, and he would take his father's metal tape measure. Then it occurred to him that the police might have locked up the house. If that was the case, he would have to measure the window from the outside, and he knew the window was too high for him to reach. What could he bring to stand on? The only thing light enough to haul all that way was the leather seat on a walking stick his dad carried in his golf bag — something called a shooting stick.

Soon he was well on his way to the Old Willson Place. This time he noticed there were a lot of new houses going up on the north edge of town. Even on Saturday trucks of all sorts lined the roads. With the new mall and all the house construction, Richford was truly booming. Casey was glad his parents had decided to buy right in the middle of Old Richford. He didn't like the idea of everything being new with no big trees or high hedges. Then again he figured these new fancy houses probably had more than one bathroom. Oh, well, when his dad finally finished the basement guest room, at least they would have two.

Walking across the frozen field was no easier than it had been the last time, but now it was daytime and it wasn't snowing, so he could see his way fine. And he could also drink in the spectacle of the woods on each side of the field covered in deep hoar-frost that sparkled in the sunlight under the bright blue sky. When he finally made it to the Willson gate, he paused for a moment, remembering his fall and the awful discovery of poor Mr. Deverell. For the thousandth time he wondered what his teacher had been doing here.

After verifying that the house was indeed locked up, Casey leaned the shooting stick under the building's big front window and lifted one foot onto it. When he tried to step up with the other foot, the seat collapsed and so did Casey. He tried kneeling on the stick, but he needed both hands to balance himself against the house. Circling the yard, he spotted an old hand plough resting against an outbuilding. Casey figured he could dig the blade of the plough into the dirt under the front window and stand with one foot on each handle. However, when he tried to move the plough, it wouldn't budge.

He went back and stood under the window, thinking he could make a pretty close estimate of the width of the window by placing the tape measure along the ground under it. When he did that, he discovered that the window was within a centimetre of what Sarah had told him the width should be. Should he let it go at that? It *had* to be this window. But Sarah had told him to be sure, and it would be crazy to go all the way out to the Sorum place if he wasn't certain Mr. Sorum or someone there had ordered the drapes.

Casey pulled out a length of the measuring tape and slid it against the house parallel to the window.

The tape arched back over him. He tried again. Now he had the end of the tape at exactly the top of the window. Keeping his eyes on where the bottom ledge of the window came on the tape, he lowered the tape and checked. There was absolutely no doubt now — this was the window!

CHAPTER ELEVEN

When Casey arrived at Kevin's house, his friend's mother was taking fresh bread out of the oven. So Casey, Jeff, Terry, and Kevin got to saw off huge hunks of great-smelling bread and spread it deep with butter and homemade strawberry jam. Casey told his three companions that the dimensions of the window matched the ones given to Vance's Draperies, so he knew they were on the right track.

Jeff was a good driver, but he was so slow and careful about everything that Casey wondered if they would ever get to their destination. Before they even got into the car, Jeff insisted on reviewing the route Casey had chosen.

"I think I know exactly where it is," Jeff said. "There's a gun club before you get to it, but it's no forty kilometres. It's more like fifty."

It was a great day for a country drive. There had been no wind all day, and the morning hoarfrost still clung to even the smallest twigs, making the passage along the roads still and beautiful. The roads themselves were well cleared through the gently rolling, snow-covered prairie. Nobody spoke for a while until Kevin said, "I hear it's been decided Mr. Hanson won't be able to stay on as mayor. People are saying your dad would run if Mr. Hanson stepped down. Will he? My parents say he'd be terrific."

"He's been thinking about it," Casey said, "and so has Mr. Ogilvy."

"My parents say Ogilvy has absolutely no chance of ever being mayor in this town," Terry said. "He's such an unpopular snob, and he has no experience except looking after his own fortune."

"Well," Casey said, willing the car to go faster, "we'll just have to see what happens."

It was four o'clock before they found the Sorum place with its high chain-link fence and TRESPASSERS WILL BE PROSECUTED sign on the gate.

"Drive on just a bit," Casey said to Jeff. When they stopped, he contemplated the situation for a few minutes.

Finally, Kevin asked, "You going in there?"

"Yeah," Casey said. "If someone comes to the door, I'll say I'm lost or something."

Casey got out of the car, walked back to the gate, waved back at his friends as he opened it, then went in, leaving the gate ajar. He was on a long driveway that ran beside a one-storey frame house painted grey with white trim around the windows. The only door he could see faced onto the driveway, which curved to the left behind the house. Casey noticed a deep, narrow path crossing in front of the house and down the other side.

Maybe the front door was that way, he thought, deciding to follow the path. From the corner he could see straight back to the side of a second building. There was no other door, but since he had gone this far he decided to keep going. All was quiet as Casey strode along the path. He was about to step out from beside the house when he heard a man's voice ask, "Is there going to be enough room in the van for all this stuff?"

Casey froze.

A second voice replied, "There will be, but it'll be a tight squeeze because we've got to pick up some boxes from Fraserville, too."

"It's a shame we have to do this," the first man said.

"Yeah, and whose fault is that?"

"All right, all right! Don't start that up again."

Casey dared a quick peek around the corner. He glimpsed the backs of two men, the open hatch of a large dark blue van, and some cartons with markings that looked the same as the ones he had seen in the Old Willson Place's attic.

"Even that night I could have talked to him," the first voice said. It had a whine in it. "At least I could have convinced him not to tell about the headquarters. *My* headquarters. At last *I* was going to be the head of a whole unit."

"You think you were going to convince him?" The second voice was full of scorn. "He was too thick to see what's going to happen to this country if groups like us don't wake people up. Someone had to shut him up."

"Well, at least they don't know who we are or where we are," the whiner said. "And in a couple of days we'll be out of here and they never *will* know."

"When this place is emptied, Elsie and I can start wiping everything down for prints and head off in the truck."

Casey carefully turned in his tracks. These men *had* to be the ones from the Hate Cell, and he knew he had to get a better look at them. He went back to where the path began, sauntered down the driveway, stopped at the door, and knocked.

"Hello!" he called out as he rapped. "Anybody home?" Nobody answered, so he headed back toward the building behind the house. The men were still busy packing the van. Obviously, they hadn't heard him knock or call out. So when he approached them, they stared at him in surprise.

"Can't you read?" the whiner squealed. "If you're not off this property in one minute, you'll regret it!"

"I can read, sir," Casey said. He tried not to look as astonished as he felt. The man he was talking to looked so much like a younger Mr. Deverell that it had to be the teacher's son. "I was just wondering if you'd like to subscribe to the *Edmonton Journal*. If you take the paper for six weeks, I'll win a new mountain bike and ..." As he talked, Casey moved so he could peer into the other half of the garage. A new red Toyota pickup was parked there.

"That left-wing rag?" the Mr. Deverell look-alike shouted. "Never! Now get out of here!"

"Hand me that crowbar," his companion muttered. "If this kid isn't gone by the count of five, he's mincemeat."

"I'm going, I'm going," Casey said, trying to calm his pounding heart. He trotted quickly up the driveway, the man with the crowbar close behind. A curtain moved, and Casey spied a woman's face in the window, a face he recognized. He started running flat out.

Jeff had the car turned around and the engine racing as Casey jumped in. "Go! Go! Go!" he cried as he slammed the door. Jeff floored the gas pedal, and the car shot away. "Boy, am I glad you had this thing ready to split," Casey gasped.

"What happened?" Kevin asked. "I saw the guy chasing you and then turn back."

"That was one of two big guys who were out at the back. They didn't want me there. I think he went back to get the van I saw. Jeff, do you know any shortcuts home?"

"For now I'll turn into the gun club and park where we can see the road." Jeff made a sharp turn at the next right and drove up the slope to the club.

"We've got enough of a lead that they probably couldn't have seen us turn in," Kevin assured his companions.

"And if they do come looking," Jeff added, "you can hide in the men's room, Casey. There's bound to be a bunch of our dad's buddies around we can talk to." He parked the car near the road.

A couple of minutes later Casey shouted, "That's the van!" He sighed with relief as the dark blue van streaked by. "Good thinking, Jeff. Now how about you drive us home a different way."

"I'll do my best, but it's going to be dark soon and I can't go too far out of the way. If it were tomorrow when daylight saving time ends, it would be even darker." Jeff drove down the gun club road toward the main road, turned in the opposite direction to the way the blue van had gone, and started the long trip back to Richford.

"Glad you studied the roads around the Sorum place like you did, Jeff," Kevin said.

"Me, too," Casey agreed.

"What did you find out?" Terry asked.

"You're not going to believe this." Casey's heart was still pounding. "One guy I saw looked just like Mr. Deverell. It's got to be his son. They were loading the van with cartons like the ones I saw at the Old Willson Place and yakking about how they were going to save the country and how they had to shut someone up. And they said they'd be leaving in a day or two."

Casey sat silently for a while. He couldn't tell them he had seen a red Toyota pickup in the garage — that was part of the investigation he wasn't supposed to know about. But he could tell them who he had seen when he glanced at the window. "Elsie Tavich was in the house."

Kevin whistled. "The woman on the poster?"

"The very same. She was staring out a window as I went by."

"Wow!" Terry said. "Now we're really getting somewhere!"

Jeff made great time and only took one wrong turn that set them back a few minutes. It was a little after five-thirty when they stopped in front of Casey's house.

"Jeff," Casey said, "you were terrific. Thanks a lot." He handed Jeff some money for the gas, got out of the car, and added, "I'll keep you all posted."

"And we won't say anything," Jeff promised, while Kevin and Terry nodded.

When Casey came in the back door, Hank asked, "Where the heck have you been, Casey?"

"Here and there. Are they home yet?"

"No. Dad phoned around five to say he and Mom got the tickets to the Oilers game, so they decided to stay in Edmonton overnight. They asked if you want a DVD player with your television. The appliance store is open Sunday, and Dad's going to call you at noon tomorrow, so you better be here."

"Yeah, I sure do want it. I'll be here."

"That wasn't the only call you got. What am I

supposed to be — your social secretary?"

"So who else?"

"Your woman friend. She said you'd know where to reach her. What's her name, anyway? Aren't you supposed to be telling me all about her?"

Casey grinned. "Her name's Sarah. I'll give her a call after I eat. What did you have for supper?"

"I ordered a pizza. Your half's in the fridge."

Casey went into the kitchen and opened the refrigerator. "Looks like the small half," he said. "More like a third."

"Well, what can I say? You should've been home."

Casey heated the pizza in the microwave and poured himself a glass of milk. It was ages since he had eaten anything, and the pizza wasn't enough. "What if I order another one?" he asked Hank from the kitchen door. "What do you want on it? Same stuff?"

"Tell them to double the mushroom topping and add Italian sausage."

"The girl says they're real busy." Casey hung up the phone and went into the living room. "It'll take over half an hour."

"Okay by me. I'm not the one who's hungry."

X X X

Sarah's Fraserville line was busy for quite a while after Casey called for the pizza, but he finally got through to her. "Sarah, have I got things to tell you!"

"Casey?" Sarah asked.

"Yeah, didn't I say?"

"No, and you sure sound a lot like whoever it is that almost always answers when I call your number. Who is he?"

"That's my brother, Hank."

"How come he's always there? Doesn't he go to school or work or something?"

Casey didn't want to be disloyal to Hank and make him sound like a loser, so he said, "He does freelance computer work for people. It's because of him, and of course you for getting the phone number, that I have things to tell."

"So tell."

"Hank found out who the phone number you gave me belongs to and where they live."

"Your brother must be pretty smart."

"Don't ever tell him that. You'll never hear the end of it. Anyway, the number belongs to Alfred Sorum. This afternoon the brother of a friend of mine took me out to the place, and I talked to two men there. One has to be Mr. Deverell's son!"

"No kidding?" Sarah was impressed. "That's really something."

"Yeah, but before I talked to them they were going on and on about how important it was that people around here came to their senses and realized that the country was being ruined — and on and on."

"And one of them bashed in Mr. D.'s skull?" Sarah asked. "Surely not his own son?"

"I don't know. Now, I've had this idea. It involves you, Sarah, and I don't know if you'll want to do it."

"Try me."

"Well, first, are you going to be in a rush to get back to university tomorrow?"

"No. There are no classes this Monday, so I'm making it a long, lazy weekend."

"Great! What would you think of going to the nursing station nearest Mr. Deverell's room at the Fraserville hospital and making a call from the station phone to the Sorum number? You're smart. You'll figure a way. If no one answers, leave a voice mail message. I know there's voice mail because I phoned the number once from the library. Or say to whoever answers the phone that you're calling from the nursing station near Mr. Deverell's room and you know they'd be happy to hear Mr. Deverell is beginning to come out of his coma. If they have a voice mail that tells them who called, they'll see it was the hospital. They'll be pretty mystified as to how you got the number and very upset about Mr. Deverell waking up. I heard them say yesterday they'll need a day or two more time before they're ready to disappear. It's very important that you don't call until after noon, and make sure you don't forget that the time changes tonight."

"Why not till after noon?" Sarah asked.

Casey heard the doorbell ring. "Wait a sec." He shouted to his brother, "Can you get the door, Hank? Here's the money."

Hank brought the pizza into the kitchen, went out to pay the delivery man, and came back. "You talking to Sarah?"

"Yes," Casey said.

"Let me ask her something."

Casey handed him the phone.

"Hi, Sarah, this is Casey's brother, Hank ... I'm a magician, eh? Well, Casey said finding your address was important. I hope you're not upset that I got it." Hank grinned. "University, huh? Interesting?" He looked thoughtful. "Maybe I'll call you sometime ... You'd like that? Well, goodbye, Sarah." He passed the phone back to Casey.

"I'll be here for your call, Sarah," Casey told her. With Hank standing right there, he couldn't go into the reason she wasn't to call before noon, but that was okay. He was sure she would do as he had asked. "Thanks for doing this."

"Sure," Sarah said. "Goodbye."

"What's going on with you two?" Hank asked. He had zapped the pizza for a few seconds while Casey was talking and was starting on a large wedge. "I think it's time, bro', that we had that little talk."

CHAPTER TWELVE

"Start from the night you found Mr. Deverell," Hank suggested.

"Well," Casey said, "you already know all the stuff I told Dad and the Mounties. And you know they graciously declined my help in solving the mystery. So —"

"My God, Casey, did you hold back something they should have known?" Hank fixed Casey with eyes so like their father's that Casey almost went into the point-by-point mode.

"Well, none of the investigators knew what the drapes I burned at the Old Willson Place looked like and that they were much, much newer than any of the coverings on the old pillows lying around the house. I figured that Richford would just sell ready-made drapes, so I thought the buyers might have gotten them made in Fraserville."

"Oh-ho! So that's why you insisted on new drapes in your room."

"I didn't insist. I asked. Anyway, Sarah's last name is Vance, as in Vance's Draperies in Fraserville. She helps in the store when she has a break, and she was on duty for Vance's big sale the day Mom and I went there. Here's what happened. Sarah recognized me from all the newspaper photos as the one who'd, well, you know, saved Mr. D. and so on. She told me she was very interested in the whole hate scene and was actually writing a paper on it for one of her classes. Well, when I found a remnant of the fabric I'd seen at the Old Willson Place, I asked her if she'd like to be part of the investigation of the whole affair, and she said —"

"Let me guess — yes. How was she supposed to help?"

"I told her I needed any information in Vance's records on who had bought that particular material."

"Really?" Hank was clearly impressed, and that pleased Casey a lot. It was never easy to impress his brother. "And did she?" Hank stopped. "Of course, she did! That address you had me search out wasn't hers. It was someone who bought the fabric!"

"It was the only person who bought that fabric other than the Bible Institute. So, of course, I had to check it out."

Hank frowned. "And Dad doesn't know about any of this?"

Casey shook his head. "There's more. This afternoon Kevin Schreiver's brother, Jeff — you know him, don't you, Hank?"

"Sure. He plays a mean game of pool. I like him."

"Well, anyway, Jeff drove us out to the Sorum place, and — oh, my gosh!" He was giving too much away. If he didn't watch it, Hank would know he knew a lot of stuff he wasn't supposed to.

"And?" Hank pressed.

"Oh, gosh, Hank, it was so exciting and I found out so much stuff." He decided to tell Hank everything — about what had happened at the Sorum house, about the man who looked like Mr. Deverell, about the conversation the two men had had, and about the cartons. He also told his brother about the new red Toyota truck in the garage and about seeing Elsie Tavich at the window.

Hank was so fascinated he had stopped eating long ago. "Oh, boy, Casey, oh, boy!" Hank went to reheat the pizza. Coming back, he asked, "Are you going to tell me there's more?"

Casey grinned. "Well, yes, there is, and it's the best part."

"Something you were just talking to Sarah about?"

"Yeah, Sarah's going to phone the Sorum place from the nursing station right by Mr. Deverell's room at the Fraserville hospital just after noon tomorrow. She's going to either tell the person who answers the call, or leave a voice mail message, that

Mr. D. has regained consciousness and she thought they'd want to know. They'll go nuts trying to figure out how the hospital had connected them with Mr. D., and I figure they'll want to check out Mr. D.'s condition for themselves, maybe make sure he doesn't come to ever."

"Are you out of your mind?"

"No," Casey told him. "Dad's going to phone at noon — he always phones exactly when he says he's going to, and I'll tell him all about everything and he'll get things in order and have the Mounties ready to capture the bad guys when they get to the hospital."

"We should phone him right now."

"Why ruin his and mom's little vacation? Anyway, they'll be at the Edmonton Oilers game until late."

Hank shook his head. "It's really against my better judgment. But, like you said, Dad always phones exactly when he says he's going to, so I guess it'll be okay. But I'm telling you, Casey. I wouldn't want to be you when Dad gets home tomorrow."

"Even if the case is solved and the bad guys are caught? He'll think I did a great job."

"Dream on, Casey. Dream on."

Casey wasn't sure if it was Hank's warning or too much pizza that kept him from sleeping that night. He was still awake at two in the morning when the time officially changed to standard, so he went through the house putting all the clocks an hour back.

X X X

At exactly fifteen minutes to eleven on Sunday morning the phone rang. Casey was enjoying a big piece of cold pizza and a cola for breakfast. He'd had a really bad night's sleep, but after a shower he had felt a little less apprehensive than when he awakened. He had gone over his plan again and again. It was going to work perfectly.

"Hello," Casey said, hoping it was his dad calling early. It wasn't. "Sarah! How's it going?"

"Going great," Sarah said. "Mission accomplished." Sarah talked so fast that Casey couldn't break in. "I did it just the way you said. It was easy to use the nursing station phone, and I got right through. A man answered, and I told him I was calling from the nursing station and I wanted him to have the good news that Mr. Deverell had regained consciousness for several brief periods and it looked as if he would soon come out of the coma for good. The man said, 'Is that a fact. And his room number is?' I heard a nurse coming along right then, so I just said 313, put the receiver down, and walked away. What now?"

"But my God, Sarah, you weren't supposed to phone until after noon!"

"It *is* after noon, Casey, forty-five minutes after to be exact."

"No, it's not. Daylight saving time ended today. It's not even eleven yet. My dad isn't calling until noon, and I've got a terrible feeling I've started something I can't stop."

"Oh, darn!" Sarah gasped. "I changed my clock the wrong way. But why is the timing so important.

You never did tell me. And what's your dad got to do with it?"

"Sarah," Casey said faintly, "I was going to tell my dad all about the drapes ordered for the Old Willson Place and how you found the number and where we found Mr. Deverell's son, and that it was all set up for you to deliver the phone message about Mr. D. coming out of the coma. I was going to tell him to alert the Mounties and have guards set up around Mr. D.'s room and to arrest whoever came looking for him. Like I told you yesterday, I'm positive they're the ones who tried to kill Mr. D. at the Old Willson Place because he knew too much. They've probably already started for the hospital, and my dad isn't going to be calling for another hour and five minutes."

"Oh, Casey, this is awful! I'm so sorry about the time. How far is the Sorum place from Fraserville? Your dad may be able to get things rolling before the guy gets to the hospital."

"It's only an hour's drive, Sarah." Casey heard something and turned. Hank was standing behind him, his hand over his mouth in dismay.

"Sarah," Casey said, "I gotta go. We've got to get in touch with my dad."

"We have to hope you can," Sarah said. "Let me know."

"Sure." Casey hung up and turned to Hank. "You heard it all?"

"Enough to know it's a very serious situation."

"But I had it all planned so perfectly. I just didn't

explain my plan to Sarah as well as I should, and she screwed things up. She changed her clock the wrong way and put in the call way too early. What am I going to do?"

"Casey, my lad, it looks like you're up to your armpits in the very deepest of doo-doo, and since I didn't insist that you tell Dad last night, I'm right in there with you. First, get the hotel number Mom left and pray they haven't checked out yet. And don't you dare blame Sarah for anything."

The hotel number was right on the phone pad. Casey punched out the number, his hands shaking. "Mr. and Mrs. Templeton's room," he practically shouted.

"One moment, please," the operator said. "The Templetons checked out about half an hour ago. Sorry."

Not nearly as sorry as I am, Casey thought as he turned to Hank. "They've checked out. Why don't we try their cell phone number?"

Hank glanced at the telephone table where a cell phone sat. "That would be great if they'd taken it with them. I guess they forgot. And we have no idea which store they're buying the TV at. So the next thing is to try to get hold of the officers on the investigation team. I've got their email addresses but not their phone numbers. I'll email them what's up and we can only hope they'll read them on a Sunday morning."

"We could alert security at the Fraserville hospital," Casey suggested.

"Good idea! You find the number and I'll call."

Casey listened as Hank tried to explain what was likely going on. Even to Casey it sounded far-fetched. He wasn't surprised when Hank turned from the phone to say, "I don't think they believe me. They say they'll keep an eye out, but they're not going to post anyone at Mr. Deverell's door or anything like that."

"Hank, we have to do something. Can we go head them off?"

"Not that, but we can try to get to the hospital before they do and be in Mr. D.'s room so they can't do anything to him. And I'll change the message on our voice mail so that when Dad calls he'll know what's up and can alert the Mounties in Fraserville if they haven't read my email messages."

"But he won't be calling for almost an hour."

"It's the best we can do," Hank said. He erased their usual voice mail message and left one telling their father what was going on. "I think I've told Dad everything he needs to know, Casey, including the address of the Sorum place. Let's get going."

"Right." Casey glanced out the window. He wished it were a day like yesterday — blue sky and sunshine. Instead, dark grey clouds pushed by a stiff north wind raced across a glowering sky. Casey struggled into a sweater, put on his coat, and zipped the front as high as it would go. Then he tied a scarf around his neck and pulled on his knitted cap, warmest lined leather gloves, and winter boots.

Hank put on his sheepskin jacket, a heavy wool

hat down low on his forehead, a long wool scarf, and high fleece-lined boots. "Lock up on your way out, Casey. I have to put some gas in the Harley and I'll honk when we're ready to roll." He handed Casey a helmet and fastened his own on.

Casey stood at the living-room window. He checked his watch. It was already well past eleven. How could the time since Sarah's call have flown so fast? A couple of minutes later he climbed behind Hank on the Harley and they were off, the motorcycle hurtling forward with a tremendous roar and a great surge of power.

"Make sure you clasp your hands tightly around me!" Hank shouted above the noise of the motorcycle and the whistle of the wind.

They were soon on the street leading to the highway to Fraserville. Casey put his head down against Hank's back. He couldn't see the road ahead. He couldn't really see anything except the icy road and all the cars that whooshed up powdered snow as they passed. Now they were on the highway, but instead of being able to make up time, they were caught in a long line of cars going both ways on the two-lane road. Sunday. Of course! People were heading home after church, or they were going into town for Sunday brunch at the Landmark Motel.

There was a widening of the road at the crossroads a few kilometres ahead, Casey remembered, then Hank would pass the line of cars and get up some speed. In about ten minutes he felt the motorcycle gathering power, dip to the left, straighten, and then blast past the row of cars until they were well ahead. If the blue van were on its way to Fraserville, it would be getting to the highway about ten kilometres farther on. Casey decided he would keep his head up and his eyes open. He did, but it was an awful lot colder that way.

The traffic was very light now, and Hank pushed the Harley hard. That meant he didn't have a chance when the front wheel of the machine hit a patch of ice, flew up, flipped once, sending Casey flying, and crashed into a snowbank. Casey lay in the snow, dazed and frightened. He tested to see if anything hurt. When everything seemed okay, he got up, first to his knees, and then to his feet. He glanced over to where the motorcycle lay. He couldn't see his brother. *Oh, my God,* he thought, *don't let Hank be hurt.* Then he called out frantically, "Hank, where are you? Hank, are you okay?"

From seemingly far away Hank's voice answered, "I'm not sure I'm okay, but God, am I glad to be alive."

Casey ran toward the voice. He still couldn't see his brother. And then he did. Well, not all of him, just the toe of one boot sticking out of a deep snowdrift. Casey dug for the rest. When he found a hand, he pulled gently, and Hank emerged slowly to a sitting position.

"I'm so glad you're all right, Hank," Casey said, stepping back. But there was something in the expression on Hank's face that stopped him. "You are, aren't you?"

"Most of me is fine, but my left hand hurts like crazy. I think I broke my wrist."

"Oh, no! I'm so sorry, Hank. I didn't mean for any of this to happen."

"Yeah, well, at least now we have two good reasons for getting to the Fraserville hospital — to look out for Mr. Deverell and to get my wrist fixed." He pushed himself up with his right hand.

"Does it really hurt a lot?"

"A lot. Now let's see how the Harley fared."

They got the machine upright and pushed it down to the road.

"Do you think it'll run?" Casey asked.

"Yeah, I think it will. The real question is, can I drive it one-handed? My left hand isn't much good."

They made a wobbly start, with the machine almost falling over and Hank yowling with pain. On the second try they were heading straight and slow along the edge of the highway when a large vehicle hurtled past. It was a dark blue van with smoked windows.

"That's the van!" Casey shouted.

"It must have been going a hundred and twenty K!" Hank hollered back. "We'll never catch up."

Ahead of them the highway curved broadly to the south. Fraserville was getting close, and the road was now four lanes wide. Hank was driving slowly, knowing there was no way they could make it to the hospital before the van. Far ahead on the right shoulder of the road the flashing beacon of a police car punctuated the gloom.

145

Casey wondered if the email messages Hank had left for the Mounties had been read. And if they had, he hoped something was being done to protect Mr. Deverell. If the bad guys killed Mr. D., it would be his fault. Casey wondered what juvenile detention would be like. He sighed, thinking of the shame he would bring on his family.

They were level with the police car now. Pulled to the side of the road ahead of the police vehicle was the dark blue van. A man stood beside it, shaking his fist at the police. The man was Mr. Deverell's son!

Casey squeezed Hank tightly. Hank nodded and revved the Harley.

"My gosh!" Casey rejoiced. "We're going to beat him, after all." He raised his eyes. "Thanks up there."

The turnoff signs for Fraserville streets had begun, and Hank headed for the centre of town. Big green-and-white H signs and arrows led them to the Fraserville hospital. When they got there, Casey pulled a parking ticket from a machine, then Hank parked, turned off the engine, and remained seated. Casey got off the motorcycle and peered at his brother. Hank's face was pure white, and beads of sweat poured down from under his helmet. He took off his left glove and showed Casey his wrist. It was dark blue and swollen twice its normal size.

"You have to get that looked at right now, Hank."

"But you can't go up to Mr. Deverell's room by yourself." Hank was on the verge of collapsing.

"Sure I can. You head into emergency. I'll check Mr. D.'s room to see if there's any hospital security there. If there isn't, I'll call down and tell them to go talk to you."

CHAPTER THIRTEEN

Casey took off his helmet and strode up to the hospital's information desk. "Please, ma'am, will you give me the number of Mr. Deverell's room?" Sarah had told him Mr. D.'s room number, but Casey couldn't remember it.

The woman behind the counter pressed various keys on her computer. "Sorry, but I'm not allowed to give out that information."

"How can I bring him flowers if I don't know his room number, ma'am?"

"Well, you can leave them at the nearest nursing station. That would be 3C."

"Thank you very much," Casey said. He pretended to walk to the Gift and Flower Shop, then turned to glance back at the information desk. The woman was talking with someone else, so Casey made his way to the bank of elevators.

There wasn't much going on at Nursing Station 3C. Casey ambled down the hallway to the left, looking at patients' names as he passed each door. Mr. Deverell's name wasn't posted, but the last room on the corridor, a room whose door was shut, didn't have a name on it. No Deverell on the other corridor, either. On that corridor there were patients' names on each door frame.

Casey returned to the room without a name and tried the door. It opened, and he went in. The room was totally empty. No bed, no beside table, nothing. But there was a second door in the room. Casey tried it. It, too, opened, and this time there was a bedside table and a bed. Lying in the bed, connected with intravenous tubes and wearing an oxygen mask, was Mr. Deverell, his head wrapped in a large white bandage.

Casey gazed at the thin figure in the bed and had to blink back tears. If his science teacher had looked bad the night Casey had rescued him, he seemed a lot worse now. There was a telephone on the bedside table. Casey lifted the receiver and pressed the number for hospital security.

"Security," someone answered.

"Sir, my name's Casey Templeton, and I'm calling from —"

"I can see where you're calling from. What I want to know is what you're doing in that room."

"Sir, if you'll just listen. Mr. Deverell's in real danger —"

"Casey Templeton, you're in real danger of being apprehended. Get out of that room ASAP."

"No, sir, I won't." Casey replaced the receiver and sat in the chair across the room from the bed. "That'll bring someone, I'll bet," he said out loud, sounding a lot more confident than he felt. About a minute later, when he heard the outer door open, he folded his arms across his chest. *Security is sure on the ball,* he thought as the door to the room flew open.

Facing Casey was the man from the dark blue van, the one who looked just like Mr. Deverell. "*You!*" the man shouted. "What are you doing here?"

"I'm here to protect Mr. Deverell from you," Casey said, standing.

The man took the few short steps across the room, grabbed the cords to Casey's coat hood, and began to pull. Casey tried to fend him off by lashing out with his helmet, but less and less air was getting to his lungs and the helmet crashed to the floor.

As Casey felt his legs give out from under him, he heard the outer door open and close. The man let go of him, and Casey staggered to a chair. Never had the sight of someone in a uniform looked so good.

"Stay where you are." The hospital security guard blocked the door as he pressed a button on his cell phone and said, "Deverell's room. Two of you. Now!" He listened for a minute, then said, "Oh, is that right? Send them up, as well." The guard stared at Casey and the Mr. Deverell look-alike. "Both of you go out to the anteroom." Casey dragged himself to his feet and limped out. "I locked the outer door," the guard said. "Stand facing that wall with your arms against it and your legs spread."

"But I'm a close relative of Mr. Deverell's," the man whined. "What's this nonsense of not letting me see him?"

"Don't talk anymore!" the guard ordered him as a key turned in the outer door and four men came in — two more guards and two Mounties, Staff Sergeant Deblo and Constable Hexall.

XXX

The clock above the elevators said one-thirty as Casey, Mr. Deverell's son, two hospital security guards, and the two Mounties got on. One guard had stayed with Mr. Deverell. Once again Casey was amazed at how fast the time had gone. Had it really taken them an hour and a half to get to Fraserville? It must have.

"This way, Casey," Constable Hexall said, pointing as the elevator stopped at the first floor. Staff Sergeant Deblo took Mr. Deverell's son the other way.

As soon as the door opened to the hospital's staff lounge, Casey found out where his dad was, and Hank, and his mom. The three of them, Hank, with his left arm in a sling, sat in chairs along one side of the comfortably furnished room, drinking coffee. Casey's mother smiled a little tentatively at Casey, Hank waved his good hand, and Chief Superintendent Templeton glowered.

"Hi, guys!" Casey said. "Real glad you got here so fast. How's your arm, Hank?"

"It's a sprain, not a break," Hank told him.

"Casey," his father said, "your mother's going to drive Hank and you back to Richford. I'll drive ahead on the Harley. While I'm setting up a conference at our house with the local Mounties and everyone involved in the official investigation, and yours, Casey, you and Hank can help your mother shop for food. Some of us haven't eaten in a very long time."

Casey nodded.

"Hank," his father continued, "come down and give me a few pointers about your machine. It's been years since I've driven a motorcycle."

They filed out of the lounge, and Casey followed his mother to the parking garage. "I didn't know Dad could drive a motorcycle, Mom."

"Your father can drive everything from a tank to a bus."

"I guess Dad's pretty upset with me, eh?"

"You don't want to know how much," his mother said, unlocking the car and sliding behind the wheel.

CHAPTER FOURTEEN

The sky was almost dark when Casey's mother turned into the Templetons' driveway, raised the garage door with the automatic opener, and drove in. Casey helped her carry all the food she had bought into the kitchen. Several cars were lined up in front of their house, including two RCMP vehicles.

Casey's father had transformed the living room into a police operations base. He stood with a black marker in his hand, writing on a huge newsprint pad hung over a ladder. Staff Sergeant Deblo was talking. Sarah was there, and next to her were Hank, Jeff, Kevin, Terry, Constable Hexall, and four other Mounties.

"Casey," his dad asked, "is there anyone not here that knows about your investigation?"

Casey told him no, but then remembered Mrs. Phipps at the library and how she had tried to look up a number when he told her it had something to do with Mr. Deverell. Casey's father glanced at Staff Sergeant Deblo, who shook his head.

"We won't need to include her," his father told him.

"Oh," Casey said, "and Mr. Sanford knows about the screws."

"The long brass screws?" his dad asked. "What about them? Never mind. You'll have a chance to tell us in a few minutes. If we think Sanford's needed, we'll call him."

Casey's father told Kevin, Terry, and Jeff that he wouldn't keep them long. He told Sarah she would have to wait until someone could drive her home. Then Chief Superintendent Templeton gestured toward the dining room. "Before we continue we'll take a few minutes for some food and coffee."

Casey was the first to reach the spread his mother had laid out: cold cuts, cheese, sliced bread, butter, and plates of brownies and cookies, as well as a big urn of coffee. His father put together a huge sandwich, poured a cup of coffee, sat down, and started in. Passing his father on the way to the table, Casey heard him mutter, "No one should ever have to be this hungry."

It seemed that everybody felt the same. His mother had to fill up the food trays twice more.

When it looked as if everyone had had enough, Casey's father said, "Take your coffee with you and sit down." He asked the four young people if they had told anyone else about helping Casey with his investigation.

"I didn't," Sarah said.

"Well, our parents know we're into something," Jeff admitted, "what with my using the car yesterday and all. But when we said it was something important and that you approved, sir, they said okay."

Casey wished he could make himself invisible.

"All right," Casey's dad continued, "I want you to listen carefully to Casey's report and see if you have anything to add. When that's done, you can go, except, as I said before, for you, Sarah. You'll have to stay until Sergeant Hexall can drive you back to Fraserville." He took his seat and turned to Casey. "You can start, son."

"Sure, Dad." Casey swallowed hard and gave a point-by-point report of everything he had done to date. There was a long silence when he finished.

Casey's father stood and faced the group. "Is there anything anyone can add to Casey's report?"

They all shook their heads.

"Jeff, Kevin, Terry," Casey's dad continued, "did either of you see or hear the men Casey talked to? Did you see the red Toyota in the garage? Did you see the woman in the window?"

"We were parked past the gate at first," Kevin said. "When Jeff turned the car around, I saw Casey being chased by one man. I didn't see another man or the red pickup or the woman."

"That's all I saw, too," Jeff said. "Just one man running after Casey. When we parked at the gun club and saw the blue van go by, we couldn't see through the smoked windows."

Terry told Casey's father the same thing.

"Well, thank you so much for coming," the chief superintendent said. "Jeff, will you drive Terry home?"

"Sure," Jeff said as the three put on their coats and headed outside.

"Tell your parents I'll be in touch with them about this very soon," Casey's dad told them as he shut the door. He then turned to Sarah. "I wonder if you'd mind waiting in the kitchen, Sarah, until the official report is over?"

"No, I don't mind," Sarah said, getting up and walking to the kitchen.

"Maybe Hank could keep Sarah company," Casey's mother suggested with a look in her eye that only Casey caught. "Hank can read the report later."

"Fine by me," Hank said as he followed Sarah into the kitchen and shut the door.

Casey's father turned to the group. "I'll summarize for you what we now know occurred prior to Casey's discovery of Mr. Deverell at the Old Willson Place. Then Staff Sergeant Deblo will report on what's gone on since."

Casey thought there likely wasn't much about the investigation he didn't know, but he was wrong.

"Point one," Casey's father began. "Mr. Deverell regained full consciousness eight days ago and has explained why he was out at the Old Willson Place and what he expected to find. He had a second operation last Friday and was under heavy sedation when you were there, Casey.

"Point two. About six months ago Mr. Deverell got a call from his sister, Eleanor Deverell Calvin, in Idaho. She told him she was worried that her son, Jason, who lived with her and ran the family gas station since his father's death, had gotten himself involved with a white supremacy group. She had accidentally on purpose overheard a phone call Jason made where he mentioned a place just outside Richford, Alberta, as ideal for setting up a ... she didn't know what, because at that point Jason realized she was listening and put down the receiver.

"Point three. Two weeks later, at the end of last August, Jason told his mother she'd better find someone else to run the gas station and that he was leaving. He didn't say why and didn't say where. But he was gone the next morning.

"Point four. More background. Jason Calvin had visited the Deverells several times as a child, and sometimes he and the Deverell boys had played at the Old Willson Place. Calvin was considered by the family to be a bully.

"Point five. Because the Old Willson Place was the only intact abandoned building anywhere near Richford, Mr. Deverell concluded that it had to be the spot Jason Calvin was talking about for his headquarters. Deverell spent a lot of evenings near the Willson Place, parking his car in a lay-by near the property and going through the house. He'd never seen anyone there, but he'd noted changes to the place. The first change was to the attic door. One day in mid-September he noticed the cross-pieces were no longer nailed on but screwed on with brass screws. Unlike Casey, he never tried the attic door. The last time he was there he noticed that new drapes had been hung." He turned to Casey. "Incidentally, I've been wondering about the drapes you burned, Casey, and was going to ask you about them. Now I know. Your turn, Staff Sergeant."

"Thank you, Chief Superintendent." Staff Sergeant Deblo took his place in front of his audience. "As you've just been told, Mr. Deverell never saw anyone at the Old Willson Place and never saw who hit him. We do know someone took his flashlight and car keys and drove his car to the Deverell garage where we found it with the keys in the ignition and the flashlight on the back seat.

"Until this afternoon we hadn't been able to track down Jason Calvin. With Casey's information we did apprehend Jason at the Fraserville hospital, but his van was empty, he had an answer to everything, and swears he has no connection with the attack or with the Old Willson Place."

"What about the phone number for the drape pickup?" Casey asked.

"Calvin swears he's just staying at the Sorum place for a few days and knows nothing about any drapes," the staff sergeant said.

"Well, what about him coming to the hospital to see Mr. Deverell?"Casey asked.

"Calvin says he didn't know his uncle was in the hospital until he got the call from the hospital this morning. He told us he was glad his uncle was getting better and had just come to visit him." The staff sergeant continued. "We sent a team to the Sorum address when Chief Superintendent Templeton phoned us. There was no one in the house, no evidence of anyone besides Calvin living there, and no new red Toyota pickup. Half of the garage floor had been freshly washed, so there were no tire marks. It would have been your word against his that you saw and heard what you did, Casey."

"Come in here for a minute, Hank," Casey's father called. When Hank entered the living room, the chief superintendent asked, "In your search for the Sorum address, did you find out anything else? Knowing you, I imagine you tried to get more information on Sorum."

Hank looked sheepish. "Well, you're right. I did try, but I found nothing."

Staff Sergeant Deblo continued, and Hank went back into the kitchen. "Our tactical team dusted the Willson attic for prints, but none they found matched the ones we took from Jason Calvin today. We believe Calvin imported all the illegal hate literature, but we don't have any proof. We believe he was behind the abusive calls we've been hearing on our wiretap at the Finegood house, but the calls were all made on public phones in different towns."

Casey sat quietly through all the questions. "Dad," he said when there was a break, "I have an idea."

"I hope it's as good as your drape caper," Constable Hexall said.

Was he hearing right? Casey asked himself. They weren't going to put him in detention? They were actually praising him?"

"Well," Casey said, "as I told you, I wondered whether someone at Sanford's Hardware might remember who'd bought the second half dozen of the long brass screws. Of course, when I checked, I took Elsie Tavich's picture, not Jason Calvin's."

Casey's father broke in. "We showed Calvin's picture to the employees of every store in town. No luck. Many said how much the picture looked like Mr. Deverell, and when they heard who he was, some said they remembered him as a kid, but not fondly."

"That's not what I was going to say, Dad. I spent a lot of time in Sanford's going over all the screws they had. Sanford's doesn't store screws the way they do it in the big box stores in Fraserville. Sanford's keeps the various-sized screws and nails in an old-fashioned sort of Lazy Susan. You look down into the compartments and slide a piece of glass toward you to get at the screws. The glass pieces are old and don't slide easily. Mr. Sanford had already put the long screws I'd ordered in one of those compartments when I went to buy them. There were six still in it when I left. Whoever bought the last six would have had to press very hard on the glass to get at them. That person's fingerprints could still be on the glass."

"Thank you, Casey," his father said, glancing at his watch. "That took rather longer than we thought it would." He turned to the four other RCMP officers, none of whom had spoken. "Now that you've been briefed, we'll be calling on you to help close this case. For now, let's have a bite more to eat."

Staff Sergeant Deblo went to the kitchen door, knocked, and called out, "Miss Vance?"

"Here," Sarah said, coming out of the kitchen with Hank, who was smiling. He looked happier than he had in months.

"Sarah," the staff sergeant said, "Constable Hexall will drive you back to Fraserville."

"Well," Sarah said, "unless it's against the law, I'd rather take up another offer I've had for a ride."

"Hank," Casey's dad said, "there's no way you're going to drive your motorcycle with that bad wrist!"

Hank held out his good wrist. "I know that, Dad. I've got the car keys from Mom. Okay?"

"Uh … um …" Casey's father spluttered.

As Hank and Sarah headed for the door, Staff Sergeant Deblo said, "Thank you for your continued discretion in this matter, Sarah. But none of this is to get into that sociology essay you're writing."

"I'm just using generalizations," Sarah said as the door started closing. "I promise."

"It's a school day tomorrow, Casey." His father wasn't smiling. "Bed!"

"Yes, sir! Good night, Officers. Good night, Mom and Dad."

"Good night, Casey." His mother looked up at him and smiled encouragingly. "Sleep well."

"Like that's possible," Casey muttered as he climbed wearily to his room.

CHAPTER FIFTEEN

The day certainly hadn't gone well. As Casey trudged home in the gathering dusk, he thought everything over. He had been late for school — a first! He had only sketched out his English assignment, praying he wouldn't be asked to read it, but he was. He hadn't even cracked open his math book, so of course there was a test. He had forgotten his lunch and hated what they were serving at the cafeteria — broccoli pizza. He had played like crazy to make the cut-off for the basketball team. Of course, he didn't.

Now he was walking home to who knew what fate, with a load of books in his backpack that made it so heavy the straps cut into his shoulders. He pounded the snow off his boots outside, removed them in the back hall, and slung his backpack to the floor. The smell of ready-to-eat spaghetti and meatballs filled the house.

"Mom?"

"Hi, Casey. I thought you'd never get home."

Casey went into the kitchen. The table was set for only two. "Where is everybody?" He was relieved that his confrontation with his father wasn't going to happen right then.

"Up in Edmonton. It's happening awfully fast, but Hank has decided he might want to go to university starting in January. He and your father went up to talk to some people. I think Hank knows his bad wrist will really slow him down at his computer. Looks like he's beginning to think ahead. And with you-know-who up there ..."

"Right." Casey brightened a bit, remembering the happy look on Hank's face last night. "Who will they be talking to?"

"I gather he'll first speak to the associate dean of science, and if that goes well, then someone in the Department of Computer Sciences. Hank's so good in both math and at the computer he shouldn't have trouble getting into computer sciences. But we'll just have to see."

"When are they coming back?"

"Hank won't be back for a couple of days. He and Dad are staying with Billy and Jake. I gather Hank and Sarah are going to some big party tomorrow night." She looked at Casey and raised her eyebrows. "Your father will be back late tomorrow afternoon.

Now wash your hands, let's eat, and tell me about your day."

By the time he had finished his third helping of spaghetti and meatballs and had gotten his mother's sympathy about all his problems, Casey was feeling a whole lot better. Finally, she said, "Don't worry about cleaning the kitchen. It seems to me you have more than enough to do."

Casey hugged her. "Thanks, Mom. I've never been so tired in my life. I think I'll have a shower, go to bed, and get up real early to study."

"Sounds like a good idea. Good night."

"Night, Mom." Casey shouldered his backpack and climbed the stairs. At the door of his bedroom he stopped. There, sitting on a stand of its own, was a television. On top of it was a DVD player. Attached to the front of the television screen was a large sheet of white newsprint. Casey glanced at the note:

Point one. You were right about the fingerprints. Jason Calvin is in custody and has admitted seeing his companion, a Maxwell Tiff, strike Mr. Deverell. A nationwide alert is out for Maxwell Tiff. Calvin has given the RCMP and the federal Department of Justice information about the hate operation. Elsie Tavich has been located and is being held for questioning. Your deductions were brilliant, Casey. Simply brilliant.

Point two. The way you handled the whole episode of the hospital visit was reckless in the extreme. Not only did you put your own life at risk but the lives of Hank and Mr. Deverell, as well. It was dangerous and thoughtless. You have, I trust, realized this and in future will think things through more carefully before you act.

Point three. Your mother and I had already bought this TV and DVD player before we called on Sunday.

Point four: Your snow removal chores are extended for another year.

A closely typed page was clipped to the bottom edge of the big sheet with a yellow Post-it affixed to it. Casey pulled it off and read: "Thought you might be interested in this assessment of what drove Jason Calvin to be such a hater, and some information on Maxwell Tiff and Elsie Tavich — Dad."

Casey sat on the edge of his bed. Who needed a shower? he asked himself as he got between the sheets in his T-shirt and shorts. He punched up the pillow behind him and flicked the remote. Yes! He was on cable! He clicked through all seventy-five channels. Casey could hardly keep his eyes open, though. Then he went back to the weather channel and saw a distressing message: "There is a ninety percent chance of heavy snowfall for the whole of east-central Alberta."

Well, he told himself, that meant there was a ten percent chance they wouldn't get the storm.

Turning off the light, he decided to read his father's report in the morning. Rolling toward the window, he realized he hadn't closed his drapes. The sky was a cloudy, rosy pink. *A red snow sky,* he groaned inwardly. *So much for the ten percent chance!*

X X X

It was only six o'clock when Casey woke up, but he couldn't get back to sleep. "I might as well read that report," he muttered, stuffing pillows behind him and pulling up the covers. The summary stated:

> From his earliest years Jason Calvin, above average in intelligence and below average in social skills, had a sense of his own superiority. When he found his ideas on white supremacy and ethnic hatred validated by hate groups on the Internet, he felt he had found a place where he belonged. The more he read and heard, the more he went to rallies and seminars, the more he believed in the rightness of the white supremacy cause. He climbed up the ladder in various associations by acts of harassment, vandalism, and violence. He was on the way to becoming one of the national and perhaps international leaders of the hate movement. Others will

take his place, but at least he and his associates are out of the picture for now. As for Maxwell Till, he's an enforcer, a goon. Not too bright but ready to obey any order given to him. Elsie Tavich, recruited while at an eastern university, is very bright and just as eager as Maxwell Till to do what is asked of her to further the white supremacy cause.

And he helped catch them! Casey thought with satisfaction.

Still, Casey knew it was going to be a long, dreary day, and if yesterday had been a bummer, today was sure to be a lot worse. He was grounded, so he couldn't go to the Halloween Party at school after all the time he had spent on his costume and after Marcie Finegood had said she would see him when the masks came off. Not only was he going to miss the party, but he had to give out candy to the little kids who came trick-or-treating because his mother and dad were going out somewhere and Hank was still away.

Casey thought he could persuade his mother that he was feeling rotten, which he definitely was, and should stay home from school. But then he realized that wasn't a good idea. She would fuss over him, make him stay in bed, and give him just tea and toast, and he had already smelled bacon and was really hungry. He dragged himself into the bathroom and had a quick shower, which made him felt better. By the time he dressed and got downstairs, his breakfast was on the table and his mother was reading the morning paper.

"Good sleep, Casey?" she asked, glancing at him questioningly.

"Okay." He downed a big glass of chilled orange juice. "I really love my TV." That was all he said except "Bye" as he bundled up for the walk to school.

At school things were just as bad as Casey thought they would be. Between classes everyone was talking about the party, even Bryan Ogilvy. He was talking about it to Marcie Finegood. Casey saw workmen bringing in the video game machines on trolleys. All the excitement of the past few weeks had drained out of him. He was really depressed and mad at the world.

Casey took his writing assignment into the library, but he couldn't concentrate and looked up at C.W. Willson's portrait with real sadness. "I'd have been such a great you," he whispered at the picture. He could have shouted it. There was nobody else in the library, not even the librarian.

He managed to get through the day hardly talking to anyone. It started to snow when he was halfway home, and the thought of all that shovelling pushed his spirits even lower. What was the use of being a real "hero" when you couldn't have any fun? Hadn't he helped solve the mystery of the Old Willson Place? Of course, he also realized he had caused a lot of people a great deal of unnecessary pain and concern.

The smallest of the trick-or-treaters started coming by at five-thirty, just after Casey's father got home. Every few minutes Casey had to run back and forth between supper and the door. He had to admit the costumes this year were fancier than he could ever remember seeing, and the number of kids seemed endless. Around seven-thirty, while he was at the door putting chocolate bars in the bags of about ten kids, Casey's parents shouted their goodbyes and went out the back way. Casey was too busy to pay any attention to them.

By eight-thirty the flow of children had dwindled to a trickle, and by nine Casey hadn't had a customer in ten minutes. He turned off the front porch light and climbed up to his room. There was lots of scary stuff on television, but he couldn't get interested enough in any one show to stick with it.

He took his "tall silk hat" from the closet, put it on, and tilted it over one eye. Casey had done a good job with it. What a shame nobody would ever see it. And the wig and moustache. And the coat, pants, vest, shirt, cravat, stick pin, and watch chain. Not to mention the mole.

Then he had a brainstorm. What if he got dressed up and went to the party, anyway? His mind raced. His parents were out, and Hank was away. With his costume on nobody would recognize him, and he could leave the party before everyone revealed who they were. It would be a gas. And who would ever know?

Casey began dressing. He didn't want to wear a coat, so he layered on the sweaters. He figured old C.W. Willson was on the stout side, so all the padding would make him even more authentic. By the time he had tied the silk scarf like a cravat and fixed it with the "diamond," put on the grey wig, and glued on the big moustache and the large black mole, he was ready to clap on his hat and leave.

The party had started long ago, and briefly he thought of taking Hank's Harley, then decided against it. Everyone in town knew that motorcycle, and besides, he really didn't know how to drive it that well. He took his bicycle instead. With the new snow the riding was hard, but it beat the long walk to his school. Casey could see the lights and hear the noise coming through the school's open front door for blocks away. He steered into the bicycle area and locked his bike in a rack — it was the only bike there.

Boy, Casey thought as he walked up the steps and into the teeming foyer, *I wouldn't have missed this for the world.* In the auditorium hundreds of people, small, medium, large, and very large, milled around tables stacked high with food and spread deep with cans of pop, taking turns at the game machines. Hundreds more, it seemed, were dancing to the wildest music Casey had ever heard. It was so great. He didn't recognize a single person except RCMP Constable Spencer in ceremonial red serge uniform but no mask, handing out soft drinks.

Casey figured the constable was doing the community relations bit. No one knew who he was, but heads started to turn as he walked by, and a buzz of appreciative laughter became a swell as more and more people tried to see what was happening.

"Well, if it isn't old Clarence Wilberforce Willson with Two Ls," said a man whose voice Casey tried to place. Casey bowed from the waist and handed him a card. The man hooted, and soon a small crowd lined up for cards. Casey, wishing he'd had Hank make more than fifty, was quickly out of them.

He tried to figure out which of the girls was Marcie Finegood, but when he looked at the hands of one he was sure was her and saw stubby black-rimmed nails, he realized it was a boy in a totally gorgeous harem costume.

Everything everyone had said about the Halloween party was true. Casey pigged out on tiny pizzas and every kind of sandwich, cake, and cookie a person could imagine.

When the music stopped, all the kids faced the stage where a huge ape, a Dutch maid, *A Wizard of Oz* Tin Man, and a large white rabbit were standing. "Time for costume prizes," the ape announced, taking off his head. "Boy, is it hot under that!"

A great roar went up from the crowd. Nobody was ever told who the people giving out prizes were going to be, and this time the choice was a popular one — Harold Maitland, the second richest man in town, owner of the Richford Mall, and all-round nice guy, even if his daughter, Greta, was a large pain in the neck.

"First prize for the most beautiful costume will now be given out," Mr. Maitland said. "If you see a Monster Elmo heading your way and Elmo taps you on the shoulder, you're *it*."

Elmo, who seemed a half metre taller than anyone else, wove among the crowd and tapped a not-
very-tall figure in a bejewelled harem costume on
the shoulder. Casey couldn't believe it. He had to
admit the costume was great, but he had recognized
the wearer. Boy, were people going to get a surprise!

On the stage the Dutch maid and the harem
dancer took off their masks at the same time. Again
the crowd roared in delight. Mrs. Phipps, the Dutch
maid and town librarian, held out the silver trophy
to Casey's friend Terry Bracco. Holding the trophy
high in one hand and his wig and mask in the other, Terry swayed in an oriental dance and followed
Mrs. Phipps off the stage.

Mr. Maitland called for quiet, then announced,
"And now Elmo will touch the winner of the scariest
costume on the shoulder."

Elmo selected someone in a gruesome, decay-
ing death mask attached to a skeleton painted on a
black body suit. When the Tin Man judge took off his
"face" and the skeleton its death mask, the crowd
got another surprise. Miss Tin Man, art teacher
Melody Schmidt, and Marcie Finegood left the stage
to the cheers of the audience, with Marcie holding
her trophy tightly.

"The final prize is for the most original costume
at this evening's Halloween party," Mr. Maitland
continued. "Elmo, do your duty."

Casey was staring around him, wondering who
Elmo would choose, when he felt a tap on the back
of his shoulder. "Not me," he whispered. "Please

not me." He turned his head. There was nothing he could do but follow Elmo to the stage, go up the steps, and stand before the large white rabbit.

"Off with your disguises," Mr. Maitland said, and Casey and the big white rabbit bared their heads.

"Casey?" the rabbit said.

"Dad?" Casey said.

Without another word Casey's father shook his head, smiled at Casey, and handed him the trophy for the most original costume. Chief Superintendent Templeton still had a smile on his face as he went down the steps of the stage to stand beside a somewhat smaller white rabbit. Casey followed him, waved when his dad gave him a high five, and went off in a daze to find Marcie. Once again someone tapped him on his shoulder.

"Unlawfully at large are we, Casey?" Constable Spencer said, grinning. "Heard you'd been grounded."

Casey shrugged. "Yeah, well …"

"Good luck," the constable said, moving on.

Casey spotted Marcie and crossed toward her, thinking, *My dad's a big white bunny rabbit having a great time at a school costume party? My dad smiling at me and not even telling me to go home?* Then he stopped and stared. *My dad, the big white bunny, dancing with my mom, the other big white bunny?*

"Congratulations, Casey," Marcie said as she came up to him. "But I think your dad should have won a prize. He's really something!"

Almost everyone had their masks off by now, and as they headed for the dance floor, Casey caught a glimpse of Greta Maitland dressed as Marie Antoinette in silver and lace and wearing a white wig. She was standing alone and seemed real unhappy. Casey pulled Marcie's hand, and they went over to her.

"Eat with us later, Greta?" Casey asked.

"Sure," Greta said, her face lighting up.

Why had he done that? Casey asked himself as he and Marcie started to dance. But he knew why. He had been an outsider so many times himself. It was an awful feeling. He saw a marvellous silver robot standing in front of a tall knight in burnished gold armour with the visor open only a crack, and a slim woman in a gorgeous butterfly costume with a black velvet mask. Casey pulled Marcie over.

"Good evening, Mr. and Mrs. Ogilvy," he said. "Having a nice time?" Then he asked, "Hey, Bryan, eat with us later?"

"Great," said Bryan, who hadn't taken his "head" off, "but how did you know it was us?"

"Just did," Casey said. *Who else in town,* he thought, *could afford those costumes?*

As they walked back to the dance floor, Marcie said, "You're setting something up, aren't you? Do you really think Greta will talk to Bryan?"

"Trust me," Casey said, "at this point Greta will talk to *anyone.* Besides, the two richest kids in town should have plenty in common." *And if Bryan and Greta hit it off,* he thought, *Bryan won't be spending so much time with you, Marcie.*

175

As the party wound down, Casey saw a white rabbit laughing with the gorgeous butterfly and a bigger white rabbit listening attentively to the knight in gold armour.

"Good," Casey said to no one in particular.

X X X

When the party was over, Casey headed out to his bicycle. He knew he wouldn't get away with this little caper. He would have to pay somehow, but he wouldn't have missed it for anything. His father had been great not to make a fuss at the party.

The snow was too deep to pedal, so Casey pushed his bike slowly through the drifts. Soon he turned his bike into the snowy driveway of his house.

His dad, the future "zero tolerance" mayor of Richford, he thought, shaking his head and chuckling. A big white bunny rabbit! Casey put away his bicycle, took out a shovel, and started to clear the driveway.

Also by
Gwen Molnar

**Animal Rap and
Far-Out Fables**
978-0-88878-368-4
$8.95

What do you do with elephants escaped from the
zoo, or whales swimming loops around in your
soup? Gwen Molnar answers these and other
puzzling questions in a rollicking collection of
readable, singable poems.

Recent Novels for Young People

Locksmith
by Nicholas Maes
978-1-55002-791-4
$11.99

For twelve-year-old master locksmith Lewis
Castorman, a dream invitation to the New York
office of renowned chemist Ernst K. Grumpel
for a lock-picking assignment quickly turns into
a nightmare when he's sent to Yellow Swamp,
Alberta, the site of a chemical spill a year earlier.
What's more, Grumpel is utterly ruthless and,
through his chemical inventions, can alter the
rules of nature. But the assignment is one that
Lewis can't refuse.

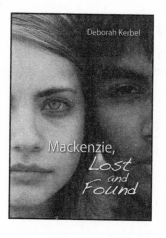

**Mackenzie,
Lost and Found**
by Deborah Kerbel
978-1-55002-852-2
$12.99

Mackenzie and her dad, alone since the death of her mother a year ago, are moving to Jerusalem, where her father has taken a position as a visiting professor. The adjustment from life in Canada to life in Israel is dramatic. But the biggest shock of all comes when Mackenzie faces the wrath of her new friends, new community, and even her own father after she begins dating a Muslim boy.

Available at your favourite bookseller.

 DUNDURN PRESS
www.dundurn.com

Tell us your story! What did you think of this book?
Join the conversation at www.definingcanada.ca/
tell-your-story by telling us what you think.